# LOVE'S ENDURING PROMISE

**Books by Janette Oke**

*Love Comes Softly*
*Love's Enduring Promise*
*Love's Long Journey*
*Once Upon a Summer*

# LOVE'S ENDURING PROMISE

The sequel to
LOVE COMES SOFTLY

JANETTE OKE

BETHANY HOUSE PUBLISHERS
Minneapolis, Minnesota 55438
A Division of Bethany Fellowship, Inc.

Copyright © 1980
Janette Oke
All rights reserved

Published by Bethany Fellowship, Inc.
6820 Auto Club Road, Minneapolis, Minnesota 55438

Printed in the United States of America

---

**Library of Congress Cataloging in Publication Data**

Oke, Janette, 1935-
   Love's enduring promise.

   Sequel to Love comes softly.
   I. Title.
PS3565.K35L68      813',54     80-22993
ISBN 0-87123-345-2

---

**Dedicated with love to**

Edward
Terry, Lavon, Lorne and Laurel
—my wonderful family

JANETTE OKE was born in Champion, Alberta, during the depression years, to a Canadian prairie farmer and his wife. She is a graduate of Mountain View Bible College in Didsbury, Alberta, where she met her husband, Edward. They were married in May of 1957, and went on to pastor churches in Indiana as well as Calgary and Edmonton, Canada.

Janette's husband is professor at Mountain View Bible College where Janette has served as treasurer. As well as maintaining the family home for their four children, three boys and one girl, she is active in the Women's Missionary Society, locally and at the district level. She also serves as a Sunday school teacher in her local church.

This is Janette's second book. Her first was *Love Comes Softly*, Bethany Fellowship, 1979.

# Table of Contents

# Chapter 1

## *New Beginnings*

Marty stirred restlessly in an effort to shake off sleep. The dream possessed her, causing an uncontrollable shiver to run through her body.

Gradually wakefulness came and with it an intense relief. She was here, safe and belonging, in her own bed.

Still, an uneasiness clung to her. It had been a horrid dream, so real and frightening; and why, she asked herself, did she even have the dream after all of these months—and so real—so very real.

She could feel it close in about her even as she thought about it. The broken wagon—the howling blizzard pulling and tearing at the flapping canvas, and she, Marty, huddled alone in a corner, vainly clasping a thin, torn blanket about her shivering body in an effort to keep warm. Her despair at being alone was more painful than the cold that sought to claim her.

"I'm gonna die," she thought, "all alone. I'm gonna die"—and then thankfully, she had awakened and had felt the warmth of her own four-poster and looked through the cabin window at a sky blessed with neon stars.

Still, she could not suppress another shiver, and as it passed through her body, a strong arm went about her, drawing her close.

She hadn't meant to waken Clark. His days had been such

busy ones, and she knew that he needed his sleep. As she studied his face in the pale light from the window, she realized that he really wasn't awake—not yet.

A flood of love washed over her. Whenever she needed assurance of his love, it was given her, even from the world of sleep; for this was not the first time that, even before he awakened, he had sensed her need and drawn her close.

Wakefulness was coming to him now. He brushed a kiss against her loose hair and whispered, "Somethin' wrong?"

"No, I'm fine," she answered. "I jest had me a frightenin' dream, thet's all. I was all alone an'—"

His arm tightened. "But yer not alone."

"No, an' Clark, I'm so glad—so glad."

As he held her close, her shivering ceased and the reality of the dream began to recede.

She reached a hand to his cheek.

"I'm fine now—really. Go back to sleep."

His fingers smoothed her hair, then gently rested on her shoulder. Marty lay quietly and in a few moments Clark's breathing assured her that he was asleep again.

Marty had control of her thoughts now. The terror of the dream had been pushed aside, so now she used the quiet moments to think through and plan for the duties of the day.

Over the winter months the community menfolk had been busy felling and skidding logs every moment they had been spared from their own work. They and their wives felt strongly the need for an area school. They knew that the only way a school would be provided for the educating of their children was to build it themselves.

It would be a simple, one-room structure, built by the creek on a piece of property donated by the Davises.

Gradually the piles of logs had grown. The men had been anxious to log-in the required number before the spring thaw, and then before the land would be beckoning to the plow, there would be time for a work bee or two.

The count had been taken—the requirement filled. Tomorrow was the day set aside for the "school raisin'." The men hoped to complete the walls and perhaps even add the rafters.

The building would then be finished through the summer as time allowed. By fall the children would have a school of their own.

Marty's thinking jumped ahead—the teacher. They still needed to find a teacher, and teachers were so difficult to find. Would they build their school only to discover that they were unable to obtain a qualified teacher? No, they must all pray—pray that the committee would be fruitful in their search; that their efforts of building would not be in vain; that a suitable teacher would be found.

Missie would not attend the school for its first term. She would be five come November and too young to join the others starting in the new school. Marty felt torn—she wanted Missie at home for another year. Still, in all the excitement over the new school, it was hard to refrain from getting involved by having a child attend. She reminded herself again that Clark and she had decided that Missie should wait—a hard decision, for Missie talked about the new school continually.

At first it had seemed so far into the future, but now here they were on the threshold of its "birthin'." The thought of it stirred Marty, and she knew that she would be unable to go back to sleep even though she should. It was too early to begin her day's work. Her moving about might waken the other members of the family.

She lay quietly sorting out in her mind what she would prepare to take for the meals on the morrow, and what would need to be done in preparation today. She mentally dressed each one of her children, and even checked off which of the neighbor women she wished to have a chat with when the work of the day would allow it.

The minutes ticked by slowly and finally her restlessness drove her quietly from her bed. She lifted herself carefully and slowly, for the child she carried made movement cumbersome.

"Jest another month," she reminded herself, "an' we will see who this be."

Missie was hoping for a baby sister but Clare didn't care. A baby was a baby to his little-boy mind; besides, a baby stayed in the house, and he, at every opportunity, went with his pa.

So Clare couldn't see a baby adding much to his world.

Marty slipped into her house-socks and wrapped a warm robe about her. The house was cold in the morning.

She went first to look in on the sleeping Missie and Clare. It was still too dark to see well, but through the light from the window their outlines assured her that they were covered and comfortable as they slept.

Marty went on to the kitchen and as quietly as possible lit the fire in the reliable old kitchen stove. Marty felt a kinship with her stove—almost like a man with his team, she reckoned. The stove and she worked together to bring warmth and sustenance to this home and family. Of all of the things that their home held, the stove, she felt, was really hers.

The fire was soon crackling, and Marty put the kettle on to boil and then filled the coffeepot. It would be awhile before the stove warmed the kitchen and the coffee began to boil, so Marty pulled her robe about her for warmth and took Clark's worn Bible from the shelf. She'd have time to read and pray before the family began to stir.

She felt especially close to God this morning. The dream had made her aware again of how much she had to be thankful for, and the anticipation of the new school added to her feeling of well-being. Only God really understood her innermost self. She was glad for the opportunity to pour it all out to Him.

Marty sat slowly sipping the hot coffee, enjoying the luxury of the liquid spreading warmth to her whole being. She felt refreshed now, both physically and spiritually. Again her eyes sought out the verse that had seemed meant just for her at this particular time. "Be strong and of a good courage, be not afraid, neither be thou dismayed; for the Lord thy God is with thee whithersoever thou goest."

It was a verse rich in promise and a comfort to her after her troubled dream. Alone. The word was a haunting one. She was so thankful that she was not alone. Again in humbleness she acknowledged the wisdom of her Father in leading her so quickly to Clark after the death of Clem. She realized now that as soon as she had healed sufficiently to be able to reach out to another, Clark was already there, eager to welcome her. Why had she fought God's provision for her with every fibre of her being? Ma Graham had said that it took time for healing, and Marty was sure that that was the reason. Given that time, she had been able to love again.

To love and be loved—to belong, to be a part of another's life—what a precious part of the divine plan.

Had she ever been able to really tell Clark all that she felt? Somehow to try to put it into words seemed never to do it justice. Oh, she tried to express it verbally, but words were so inadequate. Instead she sought to say it with her eyes, her actions; indeed, her very being responded to him in a hundred ways.

The little life within her gave a sudden jerk.

"An' you," Marty whispered, "are one more expression of our love. Not jest the creatin' of ya, but the birthin' an' the raisin'. Thet's love, too. Yer special, ya know. Special 'fore we even know who ya be. Special because yer ours—God-given. God bless ya, little 'un, an' make ya strong of body, mind, an' spirit. Might ya grow tall an' straight in every way. Make yer pa proud—an' he will be proud. Long as ya be beautiful an' strong of soul—even if yer body should be weak or yer mind crippled—jest be upright of spirit. I know yer pa. Thet's what be most important to 'im. An' to yer ma, too."

A stirring from the bedroom interrupted Marty's inner conversation with her unborn child, and a moment later Clark appeared.

"Yer up early," Marty said, welcoming him with a smile. "Couldn't you sleep either?"

"Now who could lay abed with the smell of thet coffee floatin' in the air? I declare, iffen those ladies anxious to catch themselves a man would wear the aroma of fresh-perked coffee 'stead of some Pari perfume, they jest might git somewhere."

Marty smiled and rose from her chair.

"Jest stay a sittin'." Clark put his hand on her shoulder. "I know where the cups be. Don't usually have the pleasure of a cup of coffee before chorin'. Maybe you should make this a habit."

He poured his coffee and returned to the table where he sat

across from her. He seemed to study her carefully, and Marty read love and concern in the look.

"Ya be all right?"

"Fine."

"Junior behavin'?"

Marty grinned. "When ya came out I was jest sittin' here havin' a chat with her."

"*Her*, is it?"

"Accordin' to Missie, it daren't be anythin' else."

"Had me abit worried in the night."

"Thet weren't nothin' but a silly dream."

"Wanna talk 'bout it?"

"Not much to be sayin', I guess. It was the awful feelin' of bein' alone thet frighted me so. Don't rightly know how to be sayin' it, but Clark, I'm so glad thet I never had to really be alone—even after I lost Clem. There was you an' Missie right away to fill my life. Oh, I know I shut ya out fer a time, but ya were there. An' Missie gave me someone to think about right away like. I'm so glad, Clark. So thankful to God thet He didn't even give me a choice, but jest stepped in an' took over."

Clark leaned across the table and touched her cheek. "I'm glad too, Mrs. Davis." There was teasing in his eyes, but there was love there too. "Never met another woman thet could make better coffee."

Marty playfully brushed his hand aside. "Coffee—pawsh."

Clark's eyes grew more serious. "Guess I was kinda hooked even 'fore I smelled the first potful. Never will fergit how little an' alone ya looked headin' fer thet broken-down wagon, tryin' so hard to hold yer head up when I knew thet inside ya jest wanted to die. The inside of me jest cried right along with ya. Don't s'pose there was another person there who understood yer feelin' better than I did. I ached to somehow be able to ease it fer ya."

Marty blinked away a tear. "Ya never told me thet afore. I thought thet ya were jest desperate fer someone to be a carin' fer yer young Missie."

"True, I was , an' true thet thet was what ya were s'pose to think. I tried hard fer the first couple of months to convince myself of it, too. Then I finally had to admit thet there be more to it than thet."

Marty reached out and squeezed his hand.

"Ya rascal," she said with love warming her voice.

"An' then ya up an' put me through the most miserable months of my life—wonderin' iffen ya'd ever feel the same 'bout me, or iffen ya'd jest pack yer bags an' leave. Guess I learned more 'bout prayin' in those days than I ever had afore. Learned more 'bout waitin', too."

"Oh, Clark, I didn't even know." She lifted his hand and placed a kiss on his fingers. "Guess all I can do is to try to make it up to ya now."

He rose from his chair and bent over her, placing a kiss on her forehead. "Ya know—I jest might hold ya to thet. Fer starters, how 'bout my favorite stew fer supper—thick an' chunky?"

Marty wrinkled her nose, "Man," she said, "thinks the only way to prove yer love is to pleasure his stomach."

Clark rumpled her loose hair.

"I best be gittin' to those chores or the cows will think I've fergotten 'em."

He kissed her on the nose and was gone.

# Chapter 2

## *Ponderin'*

The next morning the sun stretched and rose from its bed, scattering pink and gold upon the remaining winter snow and the whitened fir trees. It promised to be a good day. Marty breathed a prayer of thanks as she moved from her bedroom. She had been so afraid that they might have another early spring storm on the day of the school raisin', but here was a day just like she had prayed for. She apologized to her Lord for ever doubting His goodness and went quickly to the kitchen.

Clark had already left the house to do the chores and the fire that he had built spilled warmth through the farm home. Marty hurried to get the breakfast on the table.

As she worked at the stove, stirring the porridge and making the toast, a sleepy-eyed Clare appeared.

His shirt was untucked and the suspenders of his overalls were twisted and fastened incorrectly. One shoe was on but still untied and he carried the other under an arm.

"Where's Pa?" he questioned.

Marty smiled as she looked at the tousle-haired boy.

"He's chorin'," she answered; "fact is, he should be most done. Yer gonna have to hurry to git in on it this mornin'. Here, let me help."

She tucked in the shirt, fastened the suspenders correctly, and placed him on a chair to do his shoes.

"This the day?" he asked.

"Yep—this is the day. By nightfall we'll have us a school."

Clare thought about that for a while. He wasn't sure that he'd like a school, but everyone seemed so excited about it that he supposed it must be good. He only smiled.

"I better hurry," he said as he slid off the chair. "Pa needs me."

Marty smiled. Sure, she thought, Pa needs ya—needs ya to git in his way when he's feedin'; needs ya to insist on draggin' along a pail thet's too big fer ya; needs ya to slow his steps when he takes the cows back to pasture; needs ya to chatter at him all the time he's a doin'. She shook her head but the smile remained. Yeah, he needs ya—needs yer love an' yer idolizin'.

She helped Clare into a warm coat, put his hands into his mittens and his cap on his head and opened the door for him. He set out briskly to find his pa.

Marty returned to her breakfast preparations. She'd have to call Missie. Missie was a late sleeper and didn't bounce out of bed like Clare each morning, eager to see what the day held. Missie, too, liked adventure, but she was willing to wait for it until a little later in the day. Marty loved her dearly. Already she was a good little helper and was especially eager to assist Marty with the new "little sister" on the way. For Missie's sake, Marty hoped the new baby would be a girl.

She set the table for their early breakfast, wondering how many of her neighbor ladies were doing the same thing with excitement coursing through them at the thought of the new school. Their young'uns would not have to grow up ignorant just because their folks had dared to open up a new land for farming. They could grow up educated and able to take their place in the community—or other communities, if they so chose.

Marty's thoughts turned to the two Larson girls. Jedd hadn't felt that the new school was at all necessary, calling it "plain foolishness—girls not needin' edjecatin' enyway." But Mrs. Larson's eyes had silently pleaded that her girls be given a fair chance, too. They were getting older, thirteen and eleven, and they needed the schooling *now*.

As she moved about her kitchen, Marty prayed that Jedd might have a change of heart.

In the midst of her praying, she glanced out of the kitchen window and saw her *men* coming from the barn. Clark's normally long strides were restrained to accommodate the short, quick steps of little Clare. Clare hung onto the handle of a milk pail, deceiving himself into thinking that he was helping to carry the load, and chattered at Clark as he walked. Ole Bob bounded back and forth before them, assuming that he was leading the way and that without him the two would never reach their destination.

Marty swallowed a lump in her throat. Sometimes love hurt a little bit—but oh, such a precious hurt.

# Chapter 3

## *The New School*

The Davis family was the first to arrive at the site for the new school, but then they didn't have far to go, the land for the school being set aside by Clark from his own holdings. Clark unhitched the team and began to pace out the ground, pounding in stakes as he went to mark the area for the building.

Clare toddled around after him, grabbing up the hammer as soon as it was laid down, handing out stakes, and being a general help and nuisance.

An old stove had been placed in their sleigh, and Marty busied herself with preparing a fire and putting water on to heat. This stove didn't work like the one in her kitchen, but it would beat an open fire and would assist the ladies greatly in preparing a hot meal.

Missie pushed back her bonnet, enjoying the feeling of the warmth of the sun on her bare, curly head, and moved the team to a nearby clump of trees where she tied them and spread hay for their breakfast.

Soon other wagons began to arrive and the whole scene took on a lively, excited atmosphere. Children ran and squealed and chased. Even Clare was tempted away from dogging his father.

Busy women chattered and called and laughed as they

greeted one another and went about the meal preparations.

The men became very businesslike—eying logs and choosing those best suited for footings, mentally sorting the order in which the logs should come. Then the axes went to work. Muscled arms placed sure blows as chips flew, and strong backs bent and heaved in unison as heavy logs were raised and placed.

It was hard work, made lighter only by the number who shared it and the satisfaction that it would bring.

The early spring sun grew almost hot, and jackets were discarded as the work made bodies grow warm from effort.

The old stove cheerily did its duty—coffee boiled and large kettles of stew and pork and beans began to bubble, spreading the fragrance throughout the one-day camp.

A child stopped in play to sniff hungrily, and a man, heaving a giant log, thought ahead to the pleasure of stopping for the midday meal. At the stove, a woman who stirred the pot imagined her child doing sums at a yet unseen blackboard.

The sun, the logs, the laughter—but most of all, the promise—made the day a good one. They would go home weary, yet refreshed—bodies aching but spirits uplifted. Together they would accomplish great things, not just for themselves, but for future generations. They had given of themselves, and many would reap the benefits.

Maybe Ben Graham said it best as they stood gazing at the new structure before they turned their teams toward home.

"Kinda makes ya feel tall like."

# Chapter 4

# *Little Arnie*

Marty forced herself to set about getting supper. Clark would soon be in from the field and chores would not take him long.

In the sitting room Missie was busy bossing her brother, Clare.

"Not thet way—like this!" Marty heard her exclaim in disgust.

"I like it this way," Clare argued, and Marty felt sure that he'd get his own way. The boy had a stubborn streak—like her, she admitted.

She stirred a kettle to be sure that the carrots were not sticking on the bottom and crossed mechanically to the cupboard to slice some bread. She wasn't herself at all—and she knew the reason.

She glanced nervously at the clock and held her breath as another contraction took hold of her. She really must get off her feet. She hoped that Clark would hurry home.

As the contraction eased itself, Marty moved on again, placing the bread on the table and going for the butter.

She was relieved to hear the team arrive to Ole Bob's welcome, and proceed to the barn.

Clare ran through the kitchen, happy to be released from Missie's demanding play, and returned to a world where men worked together peaceably. He grabbed his jacket from a hook as he ran and excitedly shoved an arm in the wrong sleeve. He would later discover his mistake and correct it as he ran, Marty knew.

Chores did not take long and Clark was soon in, bringing a foaming pail of milk that Clare assisted in carrying.

Marty dished up the food and placed it on the table as the "menfolk" washed in the outside basin. She sank with relief into her chair at the table and waited for the others to take their places.

Clark finished the prayer and began to dish food for himself and Clare when he suddenly stopped and looked at Marty.

"What's troublin'?" he asked anxiously.

She managed a weak smile. "I think it be time."

"Time!" he exploded, setting the potatoes on the table with a clunk. "Why didn't ya be sayin' so? I'll get the Doc." He was already on his feet.

"Sit ya down an' have yer supper first," Marty told him, but he refused to do so.

"Best ya git yerself to bed. Missie, watch Clare." He turned to the little girl, "Missie, the time be close now fer the new baby. Mama needs to go to bed. Ya give Clare his supper an' then clear the table. I'm goin' fer the Doc. I won't be long, but ya'll have to care fer things 'til I git back."

Missie nodded solemnly.

"Now," Clark said, assisting Marty, "into bed fer ya and no arguin'."

Marty allowed herself to be led away. Bed was the thing that she wanted most—and second to that, she suddenly realized, was Ma Graham.

"Clark," she asked, "do we hafta get the Doc?"

" 'Course," he responded, wondering at the absurd question. "Thet's what he's here fer."

"But I'd really rather have Ma, Clark. She did fine with Clare—she could—"

"The Doc knows what to do iffen somethin' should go wrong. I know thet Ma has delivered lotsa babies, and most times everythin' goes well, but should somethin' be wrong,

Doc has the necessary know-how and equipment."

A tear slid down Marty's cheek. She had nothing against the Doc, but she wanted Ma.

"Don't be silly," she told herself; but the "want" remained, and as the next contraction seized her, the "want" grew.

Clark handed her a nightie from the peg behind the door and began to turn down the bed as she slipped out of her dress and into the soft flannel gown.

He tucked her in and assured her with a kiss that he'd be right back. Marty noted his white face and his quick, nervous movements. He left almost on the run and a moment later Marty heard the galloping hoofbeats of the saddle horse leaving the yard.

From the kitchen came the voices of the children. Missie was still bossing Clare, telling him to hurry and clean his plate and to be very quiet 'cause Mama needed to rest so that she could get the new baby sister.

Marty wished that she could sleep, but no sleep was allowed her.

Missie rather noisily cleared the table, though Marty could sense that she was trying to do it quietly. Then she busied herself with putting Clare to bed. He protested that it was not bedtime yet, but Missie refused to listen and eventually won. Clare was bedded for the night.

The moments and hours crawled by slowly. The contractions were closer together now and harder to bear.

Ole Bob barked and Marty wondered at the Doc getting there so quickly, but soon it was Ma who bent over her.

"Ya came," said Marty in disbelief and thankfulness. Tears spilled unashamedly down her cheeks. "How did ya know?"

"Clark stopped by," Ma answered. "Said ya was a needin' me."

"But I thought he was goin' fer the Doc."

"He did. The Doc will do the deliverin'. Clark said ya needed me jest fer the comfortin'." Ma smoothed back Marty's hair. "How's it goin'?"

Marty managed a smile.

"Fine—now. I don't think it'll be as long this time as with Clare."

"Prob'ly not," Ma responded. She patted Marty's arm. "I'll check on the young'uns and get things ready fer the Doc. Call iffen ya need me."

Marty nodded. "Thank ya," she said; "thank ya fer comin'. I'll be fine."

Time dragged on. Ma came and went, and then Marty was aware that more voices had joined Ma in the kitchen. The words floated on the air toward her, and then Doc was there talking to Ma in low tones and Clark was bending over her, whispering words of assurance.

Marty was hazy after that, until she heard the sharp cry of the newborn; then her senses seemed to clear.

"She's here," she said quietly, and Doc's booming voice answered.

"*He's* here. It's another fine son."

"Missie will be disappointed," Marty almost whispered, but Doc heard her.

"No one could be disappointed for long over this boy. He's a dandy," and a few minutes later the new son was placed beside her. In the light of the lamp, Marty could see that he was indeed a dandy; and love for the new wee life beside her spread through her being like a warm electric current.

Then Clark came, beaming as he gazed at his new son, placing a kiss on Marty's hair.

"Another prizewinner, ain't he now?" he said proudly. Marty nodded wearily.

Clark left, soon to return with a sleepy-eyed child in each arm. He bent down.

"Yer new brother," he said. "Look at 'im sleepin' there. Ain't he jest fine?"

Clare just looked big-eyed.

"A boy?" Missie asked, sounding incredulous. "It was s'pose to be a girl. I prayed fer a girl."

"Sometimes," Clark began slowly, "sometimes God knows better than us what is best. He knows thet what we want might not be right fer us now; so, sometimes, 'stead of givin' us what we asked Him fer, He sends instead what He knows to be best fer us. Guess this baby boy must be someone special fer God to send him instead."

Missie listened carefully; then a smile spread over her face as the baby stretched and yawned in his sleep.

"He's kinda cute, ain't he?" she whispered. "What we gonna call him, Pa?"

They named the baby Arnold Joseph and called him Little Arnie right from the first.

Clare found him a bit boring, though he would have defended him to the death. Missie fussed and mothered and wondered why she had ever felt that a sister would have been better.

Things settled down again to a routine. The crops and the gardens were planted. And the added housework kept Marty hopping, for the new baby, along with the joy, also brought more work. Marty's days were full indeed—full, but overflowing with happiness.

# Chapter 5

## *A Visit from Wanda*

Spring gave way to summer, and summer turned to fall. Little Arnie grew steadily, firmly establishing his rightful spot in the family.

Crops were harvested. Clark declared that this year's yield was the best ever.

Marty somehow managed to keep up with the produce of her garden. Having Missie's helpful hands to entertain Arnie greatly assisted her in that.

The only sadness that the fall brought was the emptiness of the new school. Over the busy summer months the men had found enough time to shingle the roof, install the windows, and put in the floor. A pot-bellied stove had been ordered and installed and simple desks had been built. The area farmers had each contributed to a pile of cordwood that stood neatly stacked in the yard. A crude shelter for the farm horses and the necessary outbuildings had been erected. Even the chalkboards were hung—but the school stood empty and silent. In spite of the diligent work done by the committee, no teacher had been found.

Marty had let tears fall silently onto her pillow more than one night because of it. It seemed so cruel that they would dream and work so hard to construct the fine little building only to have it stand vacant. Now the talk was of next year, but next year seemed such a long time to wait.

At the sound of an approaching team, Marty turned from her task of canning. Visitors were all too few and so very welcome. She wiped her hands on her apron and looked out the window to see Clark taking the team from Wanda.

They visited for a few minutes and then Wanda headed for the house. Marty was immediately aware of her vegetable-spattered apron and her work-stained hands. She threw the apron from her quickly and drew a clean one from a drawer, tying it about her as she went to the door, a smile already brightening her face.

She welcomed Wanda with a glad embrace, and both began to chatter in their eagerness for a visit.

"I'm so glad thet ya came. 'Scuse my messy kitchen. Cannin', ya know."

"Don't ya mind. I shouldn't a come at such a busy time, but I just couldn't stay away. I just had to see you, Marty."

"Don't ya ever wait fer a time thet's not busy. My land, seems all the days be busy ones, an' I sure do need me a visit fer a break now an' then."

Marty supposed that she should let Wanda spill her news, but the glow on the face before her prompted her to question further.

"But what's yer news? I can see yer fairly burstin'."

Wanda giggled—at least it was very close to a giggle, almost a girlish giggle, Marty thought. She had never seen Wanda look so happy.

"Oh, Marty!" she said. "That's right, I'm fairly bursting." Then she took a deep breath and rushed on.

"I've just been to see Dr. Watkins. I'm going to have a *baby*!"

At Marty's exultant, "Oh, Wanda!" she went on.

"Dr. Watkins says that he sees no reason why I shouldn't be able to keep this one. No reason why it shouldn't live. Cam is so excited—says our son is going to be the handsomest, the strongest, the smartest boy in the whole West."

Wanda giggled again. "And when I asked him, 'What if it were a girl?', he said she would be the prettiest, the sweetest, and the daintiest girl in the whole West. Oh, Marty, I'm so happy that I could just cry." And she did.

They cried together, unashamed of the tears of joy that trickled down their cheeks, wiping them away with hands that fairly tingled with happiness.

"I'm jest so happy fer ya, Wanda," Marty said. "An' with Doc here, everythin' will go all right, I'm jest sure. Ya'll finally have thet baby you've been wantin' so bad. When will it be?"

Wanda groaned.

"Oh, it seems so far away yet. Not until next April."

"But the months will go quickly. They always do. An' ya can have the winter months to be preparin' fer 'im. It'll make the winter sech a happy time. It'll go so fast ya'll find it hard to be a doin' all thet ya want."

"I hope so. Marty, can you show me the pattern for that sweater that Arnie was wearing last Sunday? I'd like to make one."

"Sure. Ya'll have no problem at all crochetin' thet."

Over coffee and sugar cookies, Marty and Wanda worked out the pattern—Wanda taking notes as Marty showed her the sweater and explained the crochet stitches.

The afternoon went quickly and when Arnie and Clare awoke from their naps Wanda realized that she must be on her way.

Missie was sent to ask Clark, who was busy shovelling grain from a wagon to a bin, if he would bring Wanda's team. He complied at once and with another embrace and well wishes, Wanda was sent on her way.

Marty walked toward the grain bin with Clark.

"Wanda had the best news," she enthused with great feeling in her voice. "She is finally gonna have thet baby thet she wants so badly. She's so excited. Oh, I pray thet everythin' be okay this time."

Clark's eyes took on a shine, too. Marty went on. "An' Cam says iffen it's a boy, it'll be the smartest, handsomest, and best in the West; and iffen it's a girl, the prettiest."

Clark's eyes became thoughtful.

"Ya don't know Cameron Marshall too well yet, do ya?"

"I've hardly met the man—only see'd 'im a few times at neighborhood meetin's. Why?"

Clark's eyes became even more serious.

"He's a rather strange man." He paused. "It's jest like Cam to feel thet his boy's gotta be the smartest, his girl the prettiest. Thet's like Cam." He waited a moment. "I think thet be the reason why he married Wanda. He figured thet she was the prettiest girl thet he ever laid eyes on—so she had to be 'his.' The problem with Cameron Marshall is his emphasis on 'mine's the best.' I 'member one time thet Cam saw a fine horse. He jest had to have it 'cause he figured it a little bet-ter'n eny other horse in these parts. Sold all his seed grain to git thet horse. Set him back fer years, but he had him a better lookin' horse than enybody round about. Guess he figured it was worth it.

"Ever notice his wagon? All painted up an' with extry met-al trimmin's. Could have had a bigger place to live. Men of the neighborhood figured on being neighborly a few years back and helped him log so's he could build. 'Stead, he saw thet wagon, so he sold the logs an' bought it—an' he an' Wanda still live in thet one little room. The way Cam sees it, a house belongs to the woman, not the man. Often wished thet he'd take him a notion thet he had to have the best house, too; might find 'im a way to git one. Sure would be easier fer Wanda—an' now with a baby comin', they sure do need more room."

Clark was looking off at the distant hills as he spoke. Marty had never known before what kind of a man Cameron Marshall was. She felt a helplessness concerning Wanda.

"Often wondered what would make a man feel so unsure of hisself, like, thet he had to prove hisself by gittin' *things*. Somethin' deep down must be troublin' Cam to have made 'im like he is."

Clark seemed to bring himself back from a long way off.

"Sure do hope thet the young'un be a dandy, or it's gonna be awful hard on his pa."

He smiled then.

"Didn't mean me to put a damper on yer good news. I'm sure thet Cam will have reason to be proud—an' Wanda—I'm real happy fer Wanda. It'll wake her life up to have a baby in it."

## Chapter 6

# *Marty Calls on Mrs. Larson*

The winter's day held a deep chill. As Marty packed a box with bread, soup broth, vegetables, and molasses cookies, she was thankful that no wind was blowing. The day was cold as it was, and a wind would have made it most unbearable.

Word had come that morning that Mrs. Larson was ill. It seemed that it was not a common cold or flu but something far more serious, and Marty felt that she must go and see her neighbor even though the cold held a grip on the land.

Clark hated to see her go alone, but realizing that Missie was far too young to be left in charge of Clare and Little Arnie, there was nothing for him to do but remain at home with the children.

Marty dressed as warmly as she could against the cold. Then carrying her box with her, she went out to where Clark waited with the team.

"Don't 'llow yerself to be kept over-late," he cautioned; "an' should it start to blow, head home quick-like."

Marty promised, tucked the blanket carefully around herself and started off.

The road, in the flat whiteness of the land, was hard to follow in places, so Marty gave Dan and Charlie their head and urged them on.

When the unkept Larson homestead came into view,

Marty noticed that very little smoke came from the chimney of the cabin.

No one met her in the yard to assist her with the team, so she tethered Dan and Charlie to a nearby post and hurried, with her box, to the house.

There was a stirring at an unwashed and tattered-curtained window as she approached. Her knock was answered by Clae who quietly motioned her in.

Nandry was washing dirty dishes in a pan of equally dirty water. The location of a stubby broom showed Marty that Clae had been using it in an effort to sweep the floor.

Well, at least they try, Marty thought with thankfulness. After greeting the girls, she turned to the almost cold stove. The room was cold too, and sent shivers through her in spite of the fact that she had not yet removed her coat.

She opened the lid of the stove to observe one lone piece of wet wood smoldering in the firebox, producing very little more than a thin wispy stream of smoke.

"Where be yer wood?" she asked.

Clae answered, "Is none. Pa didn't get it cut and we can't split it."

"Do ya have an axe?"

"Yeah—sort of."

Marty discovered what the "sort of" meant when she went to the scattered wood that made up their meager winter supply. Never had she seen such a dull and chipped piece of equipment. With a great deal of effort she was able to produce enough wood to get a fire going to take the chill off the house.

After she had built up the fire and placed a kettle on to boil, she went in to see Mrs. Larson.

The woman lay huddled under some blankets on a narrow bed in the second room of the small cabin. Marty felt thankful that at least clothing was not strewn all over the room. Then she realized with despair that probably everything they owned was on their backs, in an effort to protect themselves from the cold. Mrs. Larson lay white and quiet beneath the scant covers.

"Why didn't I think to bring a heavy quilt?" Marty reprimanded herself; and even as the thought went through her mind, she saw the shiver that passed through Mrs. Larson. Marty stood close to the bed, a warm hand reaching out to gently smooth the hair back from the thin, white face.

"How ya be?"

Mrs. Larson attempted an answer, but it was muted and low.

"I'll git ya some warm broth right away," Marty said, and hurried back to the kitchen to get the broth on to heat. She then went out to the sleigh and returned with the blanket that she had tucked around herself to drive over in the cold. She warmed the blanket at the stove before she took it in to Mrs. Larson and wrapped it close about the shivering body.

The broth was soon warm, and Marty asked Clae for a dish and a spoon. She took the bread from the box and handed it to the girl.

"Why don't you an' Nandry have ya some broth while it's hot, an' some bread to go with it?" she said.

The hungry looks in the girls' eyes told her that they would do so eagerly.

Marty carried the hot broth to Mrs. Larson. She realized that the woman was already too weak to feed herself and hoped that she would not object to being spoon-fed. There was no need to worry. Mrs. Larson accepted the food hungrily with thankfulness showing in her eyes.

"The girls—" she whispered.

"They're eatin'," Marty answered.

Mrs. Larson looked relieved.

Marty talked as she spooned.

"I'm so sorry thet ya be down. I didn't hear of it 'til today. Jedd should have called and let us know an' we could have been over to help sooner.

"Nice thet ya got those two fine girls to be a helpin'. When I came Nandry was washing up the dishes an' Clae a sweepin' the floor. Must be a great comfort to ya—them girls."

Mrs. Larson's eyes looked more alive. She nodded slightly. Marty knew how she loved her girls.

"Must be a real tryin' time fer ya, A woman jest hates to

git down—hates to not be a carin' fer her family. Makes one feel awful useless like, but God, He knows all 'bout how ya feel—why yer sick. There's always a reason fer His 'llowin', though we can't always see it right off like. I'm sure thet there be a good reason fer this, too. Someday, maybe we'll know why."

The broth was almost gone, but Mrs. Larson feebly waved the remainder aside. Marty didn't know if she was full or just tired. Then Mrs. Larson spoke. Slowly at first but gradually her words poured one over the other, tumbling out in quick succession in a need to be said. She breathed heavily and the effort of speaking cost her dearly, but speak she must.

"My girls," she said, "my girls never had nothin', nothin'—thet's not what I want fer my girls. Their pa, he be a good man, but he don't understand 'bout girls. I been prayin'—prayin' thet somehow God would give 'em a chance. Jest a chance, thet's all I ask fer. Me—I don't matter now. I lived my life. Yet I ain't sayin' I'm wantin' to die—I'm scared to die. I ain't been a good woman, Marty. I got no business askin' God fer nothin', but I ain't askin' it fer me—only my girls. Do ya think thet God hears my prayers, Marty? I wouldn't 'ave even dared to pray; but my girls, they need—" she broke off with a sob.

Marty's hand caressed the thin hand grasping the blanket.

" 'Course He hears," she said with deep conviction.

Mrs. Larson looked as though a great weight was being lifted from her.

"Could He show love to young'uns of a sinful woman?" Her eyes pleaded that the answer be reassuring.

"Yes," Marty said slowly. "He loves the girls, an' He will help 'em. I'm sure He will. But, Mrs. Larson, He loves you, too, an' He wants to help you. He loves ya, He truly does. I know thet ya be a sinner, but we all be no different. The Book says thet we all be a-sinnin' an' a-hangin' onto our sin like it be somethin' worthwhile keepin', but it's not. We gotta let go of it, and God will take it from us an' put it there in thet big pile of sin thet Jesus took on hisself thet day He died. It isn't our goodness thet makes us fittin' to share heaven with Him.

It's our faith. We jest—well, we jest say 'thank ya, Lord, fer dyin', an' clean me up on the inside so's I'll be fittin' fer yer heaven'—an' He will. He takes this earth-soiled soul of ourn an' He cleans and polishes it fer heaven. Thet's what He does, an' all—jest in answer to our prayer of askin'. Do ya want to pray, Mrs. Larson?"

She looked surprised. "I've never prayed. Not fer myself—jest fer my girls. I wouldn't know what to say to Him."

"Ya said it to me." Marty spoke gently. "Jest tell Him thet yer done hangin' onto yer sins—thet ya don't want to carry 'em enymore, an' would He please git rid of 'em fer ya. Then thank Him too—fer His love an' His cleanin'."

Mrs. Larson looked hesitant but then began her short prayer. The faltering words gradually gathered strength and assurance. When Marty opened her tear-washed eyes, she was met by a weak, yet confident, smile and equally teary eyes.

"He did!" Mrs. Larson exclaimed. "He did!"

Marty squeezed Mrs. Larson's hand and wiped the tears from her own cheeks.

" 'Course He did," she whispered. "An' He'll answer yer other prayer, too. I don't know how He'll manage it, but I'm sure thet He will."

She stood up. The sun was quickly moving to the west and she knew that she must be on her way home.

"Mrs. Larson, I gotta go soon. I promised Clark I'd not be late, but there be somethin' thet I want ya to know. Iffen enythin' happens to ya—an' I'm hopin' thet ya'll soon be on yer feet again—but iffen enythin' does happen, I'll do my best to see thet yer girls git thet chance."

Mrs. Larson was silent. She seemed to be holding her breath and then Marty realized that she was too deeply moved to speak—save to her newly found God.

Again her eyes filled with tears.

"Thank ya, oh, thank ya!" she said over and over.

Marty touched her hand lightly and turned to go. She must hurry home if she was to allow enough time for Clark to get back with a load of firewood and a warm quilt.

## Chapter 7

# *Exciting News*

Marty finished patching a pair of Clare's overalls and laid them aside. It was too early yet to begin supper. She let her mind slide over some of the events of the past few months.

She had gone several times to visit Mrs. Larson. Ma Graham and other neighbor ladies went often, as well, to help nurse the woman and care for the needs of the family. Though Mrs. Larson rested contentedly in her newly found peace, the woman continued to weaken, and deep down, they all knew that they were fighting a losing battle.

Marty's thoughts were pulled away from Mrs. Larson's illness to more cheerful things.

Spring would soon be upon them, and with its coming two new babies would be welcomed to their neighborhood—in April. Marty was so happy for the new mothers-to-be and prayed that all would go well.

The first to arrive would be Wanda's. She, who had already lost three children and wanted a child so badly, deserved so much to have this happiness. Now with a doctor available, Wanda had been given the confidence to try again.

"Please, God, this time let it be all right," Marty prayed many times a day.

The second baby to arrive would be Sally Anne's. This first grandchild for Ben and Ma would be very special.

Sally Anne, too, had hoped to be a mother earlier but had

not carried her first baby to full term. Now the days of her delivery were very near at hand and things seemed to be going well this time. Marty knew that Sally Anne wasn't the only one counting the days.

As Marty thought of the promise of new young lives that the month ahead would bring, her eyes lingered on her own small ones before her.

Missie was dressing a kitten in doll clothes. After much arguing and persuading on Missie's part, Marty had finally agreed to allowing one small barn cat in the house. It was named Miss Puss by Missie and treated like a baby. Never had a kitten had more love and fondling than Miss Puss. Marty wondered silently if Miss Puss would have welcomed a few moments of peace.

Clare was piling blocks in an effort to construct a barn. The blocks would periodically fall on the unfortunate pieces of broom straw that were his farm animals, and then he would need to start over again.

Arnie, who could sit alone, watched Clare intently, being particularly fascinated by the noise created when the blocks came tumbling down. This would bring gurgles of delight from Arnie as he would rock back and forth with excitement.

Clare dutifully explained to the young Arnie which straws were the horses, which the cows, the calves, and the hogs. Arnie listened wide-eyed and squealed in response.

At the sound of Ole Bob the room came alive. Clark had returned from town. Marty hadn't expected him for another hour. She got up quickly and checked the clock to see if she had misread the time. No, it was early.

Clare jumped up from his spot on the rug, warmth filling his face and voice.

"Pa's home!" he shouted, letting his building blocks fall where they might, unmindful of the damage done to the straw horses and cows.

Marty started to call him back to pick up the toys, then changed her mind. He could pick them up when he came in for supper. It was important to him now to greet his pa.

Missie, too, holding carefully the blanketed kitten, headed for the door to see Clark.

Only Arnie remained, deserted on the rug, unable as yet to get in on the family's full activity.

"Boy, I'll bet Arnie's sad!" Clare yelled as he ran through the kitchen.

"Whatcha meanin'?" Marty had to call after him to be heard.

"He can't run," the fleeing boy flung back over his shoulder and was gone, the door slamming behind him.

Marty smiled and went for Arnie.

"Are ya sad?" she asked the baby as she lifted him up.

Arnie didn't look sad—a bit puzzled at all of the sudden bustling about, but otherwise content. A happy smile spread over his face as he was lifted. Marty kissed his cheek and walked to the kitchen window.

She had expected to see Clare and Missie hitching a ride with Clark to the barn, so was surprised when all three were coming up the housepath together. The youngsters were skipping along beside their father, chattering noisily in an effort to out-talk one another.

Clark, too, seemed excited. Marty walked toward the door to meet him.

"Good news!" he fairly shouted, taking hold of her waist and whirling both her and the baby around the kitchen. Marty held on tightly to Arnie, who was enjoying the whole thing immensely.

"Sakes alive, Clark!" she said when she had caught her breath, "What's happened?"

Clark laughed and pulled her close. Young Arnie grabbed a handful of his father's shirt.

"Got great news," Clark said. "We got us a teacher."

"A teacher!"

"Yep—come fall thet there little school goin' to be bustlin' with book-learnin' and bell-ringin'. Hear thet, Missie?" He stopped to lift the little girl up and swing her around.

"We got us a teacher. Come fall ya can start ya off to school, jest like a grand lady."

"Grand ladies don't go off to school," Marty laughed. Then nearly ready to explode she caught hold of her husband's arm.

"Oh, Clark, do stop all the silliness and tell us all 'bout it. Oh, it's such wonderful news. Jest think, Missie, a teacher fer yer school. Ain't thet jest grand? Who is it, Clark, an' where does she come from?"

"He—it's a he. Mr. Wilbur Whittle is his name, an' he comes from some fancy city back East—can't recall jest now which one—but he's jest full of learnin'. Been teachin' fer eight years already, but he wanted to see the West."

Missie came to life then, the meaning of all of the excitement finally getting through to her.

"Goodie! goodie!" she shouted, clapping her hands. "I git to go to school. I'll read an' draw pictures an' everythin'."

"Me, too," said Clare.

"Not you, Clare," Missie insisted, big sister fashion. "Yer too little."

"Am not," Clare countered. "I'm 'most as big as you."

Marty wasn't sure where the argument would have ended had not Clark intervened.

"Hey," he said, sweeping up Clare, "ya'll sure 'nough go to school all right, but not yet. I need ya to help with the milkin' an' chorin' yet awhile. In a couple of years maybe I'll be able to spare ya when Arnie gits a little bigger an' can help his pa."

Clare was pacified. Let Missie go to school. He'd sacrifice. He was needed at home.

The commotion that the news stirred up was hard to control but finally it subsided. Marty placed Arnie in his chair with a piece of bread crust to chew on. Clare went with Clark to care for the horses and do the chores. Missie unbundled her kitten, explaining to it gravely that she would no longer be able to play as much. She was grown up now and would be going off to school. Then she proceeded to lay out her best frock, clean stockings, and her Sunday boots—about five and a half months prematurely.

Marty went about the supper preparations with a song in her heart. This fall they would have their new school. Missie would get the coveted education. Would Nandry and Clae be as fortunate? Marty promised herself again that she would do all in her power to see that it would happen.

# Chapter 8

## *Wanda's New Baby*

The warm April sun shone down on the earth, ridding the land of winter snow and bringing forth crocuses and dandelions. Marty revelled in the springtime sun, thinking ahead of days spent in planting her garden and tending her summer flowers.

The children now spent time outside in the sunshine. Clare went with Clark whenever it was possible, and Missie enjoyed bundling up little Arnie and taking him out to play. When she tired of caring for the baby, she would bring him back indoors and return outside to dig around in a bit of ground that she dubbed "my garden." Marty had given her a few seeds, and already a few shoots of green showed where a turnip or some lettuce was making an appearance. Missie found it difficult to leave them alone and often was admonished for digging them up to see how they were doing. Her "garden" would have been much further along but for its periodic set-backs.

Marty was about ready to ask Clark if he would turn the soil in the big garden but cautioned herself not to get into too big a rush. The nights were still cool, and early plants may yet be damaged by frost. Still, it was hard to wait.

To keep from becoming too restless waiting, Marty put

every available minute into knitting two baby shawls. One was for Wanda's new baby and one for Sally Anne's. Missie loved to watch the shawls take shape, and at one stage even added a few stitches of her own. Marty had to request that Missie restrict her stitching to such as she had been given permission to work on. Then Marty proceeded to undo the extra stitches and to set the child up with wool and needles of her own.

As Marty sat waiting for the potatoes to boil for supper, adding a few more stitches to the final shawl, Ole Bob greeted a newcomer with an awful racket. Marty had never heard him so fussed-up before. When she looked out the window at the approaching rider, she understood why. Never had she seen such agitation exhibit itself in the way that a man rode a horse. He was leaning well over the animal, using a rein as a whip and pumping with his legs as though his action could produce more speed for the animal. The horse, already lathered, was breathing hard and pushing on.

As the rider swung through the gate and straightened up, Marty could see that it was Cameron Marshall.

Clark appeared from somewhere and caught a rein as the man threw them from him and slid to the ground. He could barely stand and supported himself on the rail fence. Marty's thoughts jumped immediately to Wanda and concern filled her. She rushed from the house and met Clark and Cam coming in.

She looked to Clark, for she felt that he would know her unasked question, and he did, answering her quickly to allay her fears.

"Wanda's fine. She is in labor and Doc is there—but she is uneasy like an' she wants you. I'll hitch the team an' you can take Cam home. I'll bring his horse home later. She needs a rest now. She's already been to town an' back, an' now here."

Marty looked at the foam-flecked, worn-out creature. So this was Cam Marshall's prize horse. She didn't look very promising at the moment, but maybe Clark would be able to coax some life back into her.

"I'll be right back with the team," Clark said, and led the limping, tired animal away. Marty knew that Clark would spend many hours of the evening ahead working over the horse.

"Come inside," Marty spoke to the man before her. "I'll jest take a minute to gather a few things."

He followed, though she wondered if he was really aware of what he was doing.

"Sit down there," Marty said. She pushed the boiling potatoes toward the back of the stove. The meat in the oven gave off a delicious odor and made her feel hungry in spite of her anxious mind. She poured a cup of coffee and handed it to Cameron.

"Do ya take cream or sweetenin'?" she asked.

He shook his head. Marty wondered if he usually drank his coffee black or just couldn't be bothered to think about it.

"You drink this while I get me ready."

He did, though his mind didn't seem to be on it.

Marty hurried to the bedroom and began to put a few things in a bag. She'd have to take Arnie with her, in case the hours dragged past his feeding time. The other two she'd leave with their pa.

By the time she had put together what she needed and bundled her small son, Clark was in the kitchen talking to Cameron. Marty noticed with relief that Cam had downed the coffee. Maybe that would keep him on his feet at least.

Clark helped her to the wagon where she deposited Arnie into a small box filled with hay and placed in a corner of the wagon for the express purpose of bedding down babies. She then took her place on the seat, and Clark handed her the reins.

Cameron did not object to Marty driving the team. She was relieved over that, knowing that Clark felt that Cam in his present state of worry would push the team unnecessarily hard. Doc was already there, so Marty could drive sensibly. Even with this knowledge she urged the team forward and kept them travelling at a fairly fast pace. Wanda had asked for her. She planned to be there if she could.

By the time they had reached the Marshalls' one-room cabin, Cameron had settled down and seemed again to be in possession of himself.

He helped Marty from the wagon, handed her Arnie, and placed her bag of belongings on the ground, promising to bring it in for her upon his return from caring for the team.

Marty hurried in. She placed Arnie on the floor on her coat, promising herself that she would later see to having the box with its hay mattress brought from the wagon for him.

She crossed to the bed at the far end of the one room. Doc paid little heed to her, for Wanda was getting his full attention.

"May I talk to her?" Marty whispered.

"Go ahead," he answered. "Quiet her if you can."

Marty nodded. She slipped to the head of the bed and looked down at Wanda's pale face.

"I'm here," she said softly.

Wanda brightened some. "You came. I'm so glad. I'm scared, Marty. What if—?", but Marty didn't let her finish.

"Everythin' is goin' jest fine," she said. "Doc is here. Shouldn't be long now 'til ya have thet fine son—or pretty daughter, thet ya been a wantin'. Jest ya take it easy an' listen careful to what Doc tells ya to do. He knows all 'bout birthin' babies."

Wanda looked convinced.

"I'll try."

"Good! Now I'm gonna git yer man an' the Doc some supper. 'Member I'm right here iffen ya need me."

Wanda gave a slight nod, then closed her eyes again.

Marty squeezed her hand and left her to see what she could find to go with the meat and loaf of bread that she had brought along for their supper. She was thankful that Arnie slept.

Supper was prepared and partaken of. Doc took a moment from his vigil to gulp a cup of coffee and eat a cold meat sandwich. Marty could read worry in his face. It unnerved her and made her fumbly as she cleared the table and washed up the dishes.

The one small room seemed overcrowded with people and anxiety. Cameron left to pace back and forth beneath the stars. Marty found a moment to whisper an inquiry to the Doc.

"She should have delivered by now," he answered honestly. "I don't like it. The baby is small and sure doesn't need that added struggle to get into the world. I'm afraid that the extra time will weaken it. I'm thinking of sending for Mrs. Graham. I hope I'm wrong, but I'm afraid that once that baby's here, it's going to take all that we've got to keep it with us."

Marty prayed a silent prayer, the tears flooding her eyes.

"I'll send Cam," she said.

She carefully removed all traces of her tears. There was no need to alarm Cameron further. She went out into the cool night and found him sitting, head in hands, on the chopping block.

"Cam," Marty said. He looked up worriedly.

"Doc says he'd like to have Ma Graham here, jest as an extry like, so's one can sorta look to Wanda an' the other care for the baby when it comes. Doctors like to work with assistants like, an' me, I know nothin' 'bout deliverin' babies. Ya can take the team. Doc says there's lots of time."

Cameron got to his feet. He seemed to be relieved there was something he could do.

Marty returned to the house and listened for the team to leave the yard.

"Good," she thought, "he's drivin' sensibly."

The long night dragged on. Cameron and Ma arrived and Ma relieved the doctor while he had a cup of coffee and then stretched a bit, walking around the farmyard.

Marty made more coffee, consoled Wanda, and fed Arnie. There was no place to lie down. She looked at Arnie in his hay-filled box and envied him.

Finally, just after the new day had poured its dawn over the eastern horizon, the new baby made his appearance. Marty had gone to the woodpile to replenish the fire and upon her return she heard the weak cry of a newborn.

Wanda, too, heard the cry and a glad murmur came from her pale lips.

"It's a boy," the doctor announced in the triumphant voice that a doctor uses on such occasions, but as he looked at the tiny baby he knew that a fight lay before him. The baby was so very weak from his battle to be delivered that the doctor feared every breath might be his last.

He nodded to Ma to take over with Wanda and carried the fragile bundle to the table.

Marty was given orders to push the table nearer to the stove and spread the small blankets to receive the little one; and there, with his satchel opened beside him, the Doc took on a battle for life that would last for many hours.

Every bit of his training and available medication was called upon to assist in the fight. Twice he thought that he had surely lost, but somehow a spark of life was again coaxed into the tiny body.

And so it was, that twenty-eight hours later, when Marty and the doctor left for home, Wanda still had her baby boy, and Cameron's eyes spoke volumes regarding his thankfulness and appreciation. He even promised Doc his horse in payment for his services.

Ma remained to spend the days with Wanda until she was able to be on her feet again. Cameron took a couple of blankets to the hayloft for himself, and spread a feather tick on the cabin floor for Ma.

Already Cameron was making boastful comments about the boy that his son would become and of the great things that they would accomplish together.

Marty returned home so weary that she could hardly guide the horses. Good old Dan and Charlie, given their head, found their own way at their own pace.

Clark welcomed Marty when she drove into the yard, as did two excited children and a half-wild dog. Marty fairly dropped herself into Clark's arms.

"It's a boy," she said, "an' he's livin'. Doc says thet he should make it now."

Marty reached her bed with little Arnie. She held him close as she nursed him. He had been such a good baby through the whole ordeal. She kissed his soft head and then sleep claimed her. Clark found them thus. The contented baby, playing with bare toes and talking to himself, and the tired mother sound asleep.

## Chapter 9

# *Mrs. Larson*

The month of April not only brought new life into the neighborhood, but it also claimed life as well. Word came to Clark and Marty on a rainy Wednesday afternoon that Mrs. Larson had quietly slipped away in her sleep.

Marty sorrowed that Clae had been the one to find her. The poor girl should have been spared that much at least, but Jedd had not been home at the time.

The funeral was planned for the next day. The neighbor men built the plain wooden box in which the body was laid after the women had carefully bathed and prepared it for burial. Marty took one of her own dresses to lay Tina Larson to rest in, and Mrs. Stern spared a blanket to drape the inside of the coffin.

The rain made the digging of the grave a miserable task, but all was in readiness by the appointed time.

At two in the afternoon the wagons slowly made their way to a sheltered corner of Jedd's land where a short service of committal was performed. Clark and Ben Graham were in charge.

Marty's heart ached for the two girls standing huddled together in the rain as they watched their only source of love and comfort lowered into the ground. She dared to go to Jedd after the service and suggest that she would be glad to take the girls home with her for a few days until things were "sorted out."

"Be no need," he answered her. "There be plenty to home to keep their minds an' hands busy."

Marty felt anger rise sharply within her and turned away quickly to keep from expressing it. She wouldn't forget her promise to Tina Larson and would fight as long as she could to fulfill it—yet how was it ever to be accomplished? School would be starting in the fall and somehow those two girls must be there. She'd pray harder. God had mysterious ways of answering prayer, beyond man's imagination. She bit her lip to stop its quivering, wiped the tears that were mingling with the rain on her cheeks, and went to join Clark, who was waiting in the wagon.

# Chapter 10

## *Plottin' an' Plannin'*

The death of Mrs. Larson was still on Marty's mind. She could not rid herself of a feeling of heaviness for the girls. She knew that the poor little things were trying to cope with a situation too big even for an adult.

She had visited the girls twice in the days following the funeral, taking fresh baking, vegetables and cold meat. Still her heart ached within her each time she thought about them. She decided that a visit to Ma was what she needed. Ma could help her think this thing through and come up with something that would help her persuade the stubborn Jedd to allow the girls their schooling.

Marty had come to know the girls much better in the days of Mrs. Larson's illness. Nandry was the older of the two and was quiet and withdrawn. Marty feared that even now it might be too late to help Nandry come out of her shell and develop into a young lady capable of self-expression and self-worth. Clae was like a small flower kept out of the sunshine. Given a chance, she felt confident that Clae could burst forth into full bloom. Gradually Clae had lost her shyness with Marty, and Marty noticed that even though she was the younger, it was Clae who often took the lead.

Marty set her chin determinedly. Somehow she must get that promised chance for those girls. At breakfast she approached Clark.

"It bein' sech a fine day, I thought I'd give the young'uns some air an' pay a visit to Ma."

"Fine," he responded. "Grounds not dry 'nough fer seedin' today. Ya can take the team. I'm gonna spend me the day cleanin' more seed grain jest in case it drys 'nough to plant the lower field this spring. I'll bring ya the team whenever yer ready."

"Should be all set in 'bout an hour's time," Marty answered. "It'll be right good to have a chat with Ma. She hasn't been home from Wanda's fer too long. I'll be able to hear all 'bout how thet new boy be doin'."

"An'—" Clark prompted.

"An'—I'll maybe give her a chance to talk 'bout thet comin' baby of Sally Anne's. 'Magine she's gittin' right uptight waitin' on thet one; it already bein' on the late side."

"An'—" Clark said again.

Marty looked at him. Okay—so he knew that neither of those reasons was the real purpose for her calling on Ma. She sighed.

"I wanna talk to her 'bout the Larson girls. Clark, somethin' jest got to be done 'bout 'em, but I'm not smart 'nough to figure out what."

Clark pushed aside his empty porridge bowl and rose to get the coffeepot. He poured Marty a second cup and then refilled his own and returned the pot to the stove.

So that's it, his eyes seemed to say, but he sipped the coffee silently. Finally he spoke.

"Jedd Larson be a mite bullheaded. Seems unless he decides thet his young'uns need thet edjecation, there not be much hope of enyone changin' his mind."

"I know thet. Oh, I wish thet I had me some way of persuadin' 'im. Do ya think thet you talkin' to 'im as a man might help?"

Clark shook his head.

"Jedd never did listen much to my say so."

"It's mean," Marty stormed, "jest plain mean."

"Don't fergit thet those girls git his meals an' wash his clothes."

"It's still not fair."

"Maybe ya'll have to pray the Lord to send on a new Mrs. Larson." Clark's eyes twinkled but Marty's flashed.

"I wouldn't pray thet on eny woman—no matter how ill I thought of her."

Clark just smiled and rose to his feet.

"Don't know of eny other way out," he said. "I'll have the team waitin'. C'mon, Clare, let's go git the horses ready. You too, Arnie, c'mon with yer pa."

The boys both responded to the offer—Clare with a bound toward the door and Arnie holding up his arms to be carried.

Marty hastened to clear the table and do up the dishes. Missie decided that it was her turn to wash and thus slowed down the procedure, but Marty knew that it was worth the extra time to encourage her helpfulness.

Ma was glad to see them and hurried them into the house where her children welcomed the Davis youngsters and took them off to play. Nellie volunteered to entertain young Arnie, and Marty accepted her offer gratefully.

Ma and Marty sat down to a cup of coffee, warm nut bread, and a welcome chat.

"How's thet new boy of Wanda's?"

"Tiny—but he's a spunky little 'un. He's got a lot of fight in 'im fer sure."

"What did they finally name 'im?" Marty smiled, remembering the long list of names that Cam and Wanda were trying to choose from.

"Everett Cameron DeWinton John."

"Quite a handle fer sech a small bundle."

"Seems so, but maybe someday he'll fit it."

"I'm so glad he's okay," Marty said with feeling. "It would have crushed poor Wanda iffen she'd lost another baby."

Ma agreed.

"How's Sally Anne?"

"She's fine, but she sure be tired of waitin'. Ya know how it can seem ferever. I called over to see her yesterday. Even got the cradle thet Jason made all laid with blankets, an' she's jest a achin' to fill thet little bed up. Still I don't think thet the time be a settin' as heavy on her as on her ma. I never dreamed thet I'd ever git so flustered-like over the comin' of a ·young'un.''

"Are ya gonna deliver her?"

"Land sakes no! We're gittin' the Doc fer sure fer thet one. Funny thing—me havin' delivered so many young'uns in my time, but jest a thinkin' on thet 'un makes me feel as skitterish as a yearlin' first time in harness. We's all set to send Tommie off fer Doc at the first warnin'. I'll sure be glad-like when it's all over."

Marty nodded. She'd be glad, too. She wondered what it would be like to see your own daughter about to give birth. Must be a mite scary—knowing the pain but unable to share it. She reckoned that when it was Missie's turn, she'd be even more nervous than Ma. She pushed the thought from her and changed the subject.

"Ma, I really came 'bout somethin' else. Ya know thet I promised Tina Larson thet I'd do all I could to see thet Nandry and Clae had a chance fer their schoolin', an' Jedd— well, I jest fear thet he won't be 'llowin' no sech thing. In jest a few months now thet schoolhouse will be openin' its door, an' Jedd Larson declares thet no daughter of his be a needin' it."

Marty looked at Ma, the helplessness showing in her eyes.

"What we gonna do to make 'im change his mind?"

"Reckon there ain't much of enythin' thet will make Jedd Larson change his mind, lessen he wants to. Me, I wouldn't even be knowin' where to begin to work on thet man. He ain't got 'im much of a mind, but what he has got sure can stay put.''

"Yeah," Marty sighed and played with her coffee cup. There didn't seem to be much hope for her to keep her promise. What could she do? She had prayed and prayed, but Jedd did not seem to be softening in the slightest toward the idea of schooling for his girls. Well, she'd just have to pray some more. Maybe somehow the Lord could open the mind of that stubborn man.

As she helped Ma gather up the dishes, an excited Jason arrived at the door.

"Ma," he called, rushing in without a knock or a howdy, "Sally Anne thinks it be time."

"Tom's in the field by the barn," Ma told him all in a flurry; "send 'im fer Doc and you come back with me." She grabbed a bag from a corner shelf, threw her shawl about her shoulders, and left the house almost on a run.

It was only then that Marty realized that the bag in the corner had been all packed and ready to go.

Tom left the yard on a galloping horse, and Ma and Jason left at not much slower a pace in his wagon.

Marty bundled her small family and headed for home. She was sure that all would go well for Sally Anne and her baby; still, she found herself praying as she travelled.

Later that afternoon Tom was sent over with the glad news that Sally Anne was safely delivered of a small daughter and that Grandma and Grandpa were holding up fine.

"Jest think," he said proudly, "I'm Uncle Tom now. Guess I'll have to go out an' git me a cabin."

Marty smiled.

"What ya mean?" Missie queried. "Can't ya live at home when yer an uncle?"

Tom winked at Marty. "Yeah," he said, "guess I can. Guess they won't kick me out jest 'cause I'm an uncle. 'Specially when I'm an uncle who does most of the chorin'. Won't need me thet cabin fer a while. Enyway I'm not in the mood fer batchin'. I'll wait 'til I git me a cook 'fore I go movin' into a cabin of my own."

Marty awakened to an awareness that young Tommie was indeed growing up, and perhaps his jesting about a cabin of his own had more serious meaning than he pretended. How quickly they grew up and changed, these young ones.

Her mind checked the girls of the neighborhood. Would any of them be good enough for young Tom Graham who had so endeared himself to her when he had cheerfully done Clark's chores and spent his evenings reading to the young Missie? Now he stood before her on the threshold of manhood. Marty hoped that when the time came for him to take a bride, he would find one worthy of him.

Tom sat bouncing Arnie on his foot and went back to the subject of his new niece.

"They still haven't decided fer sure on her name. Sally Anne wants to call her Laura, but Jason be holdin' out fer Elizabeth. Seems he read 'im a story 'bout an Elizabeth, an' always wanted a daughter by thet name. Then he insists thet she should have Sally or Anne in her name too. Elizabeth Sally sounds kinda funny. Me, I'm a favorin' Elizabeth Anne. What ya think?"

"I like it," Marty assured him. "I think it's a right pretty name."

"Me too," Missie joined in, anxious to share her opinion and make her presence known to her beloved Tom.

"Thet should settle it then," he said. "I'll jest tell Sally Anne thet Missie says it should be Elizabeth Anne, so Elizabeth Anne it must be."

Missie grinned shyly.

Tom placed little Arnie on the floor and prepared to take his leave.

"I best be gittin'. Nellie will be mad iffen I'm late fer supper, an' there's still the chorin' to do. Don't s'pose I'll git much help from 'Grandpa' tonight."

He enjoyed his teasing. Marty smiled.

"Tell 'Grandpa' thet we send our love," she said.

With a nod and a wave of his hand he was off.

"I like 'im," Missie whispered. "I think when I grow up I'll marry Tommie."

"My land, child!" Marty exclaimed. "Ya not yet six an' talkin' of marryin'. Let's not rush things quite so much, okay?"

"I didn't mean now," Missie explained. "I said when I grow up. First, I gotta go to school."

# Chapter 11

## *A Strange Answer*

Spring reluctantly gave way to summer. The garden produced its crops and the warm summer sun began to be hot and difficult to bear. Marty was glad for the cool breezes that blew off the distant hills. But soon summer too would be gone, and fall would be upon them. With the fall would come preparations for school. Correspondence with Mr. Wilbur Whittle assured them that he had not changed his mind and would be arriving in late August to acquaint himself with the people and the area, and to prepare the schoolroom for the commencement of classes.

Arrangements had been made for him to board at the Watleys, and Mrs. Watley had her two grown-up daughters polishing themselves as well as the family silver.

Missie was counting the days. Her whole life was now filled with thinking of the new school year. What she would wear, what she would learn, who she would play with were all very important in her daily planning.

She had two deep regrets. One was that Miss Puss would need to put in long days alone in her absence, and the second was that Tommie declared himself to be too old to attend school with all the neighborhood youngsters. She'd miss Tommie. She wanted so much to have him there. She would be so proud to stand and recite a well-learned lesson if Tommie were listening. She would work extra hard at her reading and sums if he were there to observe her skills. But Tom was not to be there and Missie, though still excited about the prospect of school, felt disappointment.

Marty too was disappointed—not over Tom but over the Larson girls. The school term was only a few weeks away, and there had been no change in Jedd Larson's attitude. Marty was about to concede that her prayers had been in vain.

At the pre-breakfast prayer time Marty was mulling over these thoughts in her mind as Clark read the morning scripture, "Ask an' it shall be given you; seek—"

"I been askin', Lord, an' nothin' been happenin'," she admonished her Lord and immediately felt guilt and remorse.

"I'm sorry, Father," she said in her thoughts. "I guess I'm 'bout the most faithless an' impatient child thet ya got. Help me to be content-like an' to keep on havin' faith."

Clark seemed to sense her mood and in his morning prayer included this petition: "An', Lord, ya know thet 'fore long now our school will be a startin' an' ya know how Marty promised Mrs. Larson to try an' see thet the girls got their schoolin'. Only you can work in Jedd's heart to let her keep thet promise, Lord. We leave it to you to work out in yer own good way and time."

Marty silently thanked Clark for his caring. Maybe now God would act. He often did when Clark prayed. She immediately reprimanded herself. True, Clark seemed blessed with answered prayers, but she was God's child, too; and the Bible said that God did not regard one of His children above the other. If Clark's prayers were answered more frequently, it was because Clark had more faith. She determined to exercise her faith more.

Later in the day Ole Bob announced an approaching team. To Marty's surprise it was Jedd Larson. It had been some months since Jedd had been over, and Marty could sense an answer to prayer.

Clark met Jedd outside and they talked neighbor fashion while Jedd tied the horses to the rail fence.

Marty put on the coffeepot and cut pieces of gingerbread.

"I wonder jest how he'll say it without backin' down none."

Jedd and Clark were soon in and seated, and Marty fairly held her breath waiting for Jedd to spill the good news. He brought news all right—news that made him grin from ear to ear—but hardly what Marty had been expecting.

"Sold me my farm yesterday."

Clark looked up in surprise.

"Ya did? Someone local?"

"Nope—new guy jest come in. He was with thet wagon train thet's goin' through—had planned to go further west, but his Missus took sick. Decided to stay on here. I showed 'im my farm and he offered me cash—outright. Good price, too."

Jedd stopped to let his good fortune take effect on his hearers. Then went on.

"The train's restin' fer a couple of days 'fore goin' on. I'm thinkin' a takin' his spot with the train. Al'ays did want to see what was further on; never can tell—might find me gold or sumpin'."

Marty finally drew a breath.

"What 'bout the girls?" she said.

She knew that it was a foolish question. All hope now of keeping her promise seemed to be vanishing. If Jedd was moving away, there would be no hope of the girls ever getting any schooling.

Jedd answered, "What 'bout the girls? Wagon-trainin' won't hurt 'em none. Do 'em good to see more of the country."

"But—but they be so young."

Marty stopped. Something within her warned her to be silent, but she suddenly felt sick to her stomach as all her hopes and unanswered prayers came crashing down about her.

Jedd looked at her evenly, but said nothing. He then reached for another piece of gingerbread and went on as though Marty had never spoken.

"This new man—name's Zeke LaHaye. Seemed to like the looks of my land real good—paid me a first-rate price fer it. He's got 'im three young'uns—a near-growed girl an' two young boys."

"Thet right?" Clark responded. "Guess I should pay me a call on 'em. Might want to send his young'uns to school."

Jedd snorted.

"Don't know why he'd do a fool thing like thet. Both of those boys be big enough to git some work out of. Must be around twelve an' eight I'd say. An' thet daughter be almost of an age to take on a home of her own. I be thinkin' myself thet she might be right handy to have along goin' West."

He grinned a lecherous grin. Marty felt her stomach sicken. Clark humored the man.

"S'pose," he said slowly, "thet a young good-lookin' buck like you be takin' another bride 'fore ya know it."

He winked at Jedd, and Marty felt hot anger raise against him. Clark looked thoughtful, then broke the silence.

"Ya know I'm a thinkin' thet when it comes to marryin' agin a young woman might think twice 'bout takin' on two near-growed girls. 'Course an older, more sensible-like woman might not mind. Ya could always do thet—take ya an older, settled one 'stead of some flighty, pretty young thing. Might not be as much fun but. . ."

Clark was silent, and it was obvious by the look on Jedd's face that he was thinking on the words.

"Ya could leave the girls here I s'pose, so's they wouldn't slow ya down none, either in yer travel, or any other way."

Clark gave Jedd a playful jab with his elbow. Jedd grinned.

"Hadn't thought of thet," he deliberated, "but those new folk gonna move into my house—hafta have everythin' all cleared out tomorra. Don't s'pose they want the girls hangin' on."

"Thet's tough," said Clark and appeared to really be working on Jedd's problem. "Kinda puts a man at a disadvantage-like, don't it?"

Jedd looked worried. Marty wished that she could excuse herself and go be sick. Never had Clark made her so angry—or so puzzled. To sit there feeding the ego of this, this disgusting person and disposing of his two daughters as though they were unwanted baggage made her so upset that she feared at any moment she might explode.

Clark seemed to have suddenly thought of something.

"S'pose ya could put 'em up here fer a while. We do have us an extry bedroom. Might jest be able to make room."

So that was it. Marty's climbing temper began to recede. Clark was using Jedd's self-image as a male of desirable qualities to try to fight for the girls. He was offering to keep them. Marty wondered why she hadn't thought of it. She sent Clark a quick glance to show him that she now understood and to implore him to please, please fight.

Jedd rubbed his grizzly chin.

"Thet right?"

"I think we could manage—'til ya got kinda settled-like," Clark grinned and jabbed with his elbow again.

Jedd appeared to be thinking carefully.

" 'Course," Clark continued, "Marty has the say of the house an' how crowded-in she wants us. Sorta up to her."

Marty wanted to cry out, "Oh, please, please, Jedd," but instead she took her cue from Clark, and even surprised herself at her nonchalant empty-sounding voice.

"S'pose we could—fer a while—iffen it'll help ya out some."

"Might do," Jedd finally said. "Yeah, might do."

Marty didn't dare look up. The hot tears in her eyes threatened to spill into her coffee cup. She quickly left the table on the pretense of tending to the fire. When she had herself somewhat under control, she poured the men another cup of coffee and then went to her room where she leaned against the cool window ledge and prayed God to please forgive her lack of faith and to please help Clark in the battle he was presently engaged in.

A few moments later Clark came in, gave her shoulder a quick squeeze, and rummaged in a drawer, then was gone.

Marty heard the men leave the house, and in a short time Jedd's team was on its way out of the yard.

Clark returned to the bedroom and gently turned Marty to face him. Her tear-filled eyes looked into his and she hardly dared voice the question.

"Did he—?"

"Did he agree? Yeah, he agreed."

Her tears started again.

"Oh, Clark, thank ya," she said when she was able to speak. "I never, ever thought thet I'd be able to have the girls right here." She sniffed and Clark pulled out his handkerchief. It was man-sized, but Marty blew. "Thank ya," she said again. Suddenly her eyes snapped, "At first I was so mad, you a talkin' thet way to thet—thet conceited—" she sputtered, knowing that she should not voice the words that she was thinking.

"I couldn't imagine why ya'd say sech things 'til—'til I began to see—. An' he believed it all, didn't he? Believed thet a woman—a young woman—in her right mind would take to him."

She was getting angry again at the very thought of it all, so she decided to change the subject before she worked herself up.

"An' he said thet we could take the girls?"

"Yep."

"To keep?"

"Well, he didn't exactly say fer how long, but I'll be very surprised iffen Jedd Larson ever wants his girls back. He'll git hisself all tied up in this or thet, an' his girls won't enter much into his thinkin'."

Marty had a sudden thought that she knew she shouldn't express, yet she felt that she needed an answer.

"Ya didn't make 'im pay their keep, did ya?"

Clark grinned at that.

"Well—not exactly," he said slowly.

"Meanin'?"

"Jedd said thet we could keep the girls iffen we gave 'im ten dollars a piece fer 'em."

Marty pulled back. "Well, I never!" she snorted. "I never thought thet I'd live to see the day thet one had to pay fer the privilege of feedin' an' clothin' another man's young'uns."

Clark pulled her back against him and smoothed the long brown hair as though by so doing he could smooth her overwrought nerves, but when he spoke there was humor in his voice.

"Now, now," he said as though to an angry child, "ya wanted yer prayers answered, didn't ya? Who are we to quibble as to how it be done?"

Marty relaxed in his arms. He was right of course. She should be feeling thankfulness, not frustration.

"The girls will be here tomorrow. It's gonna be strange fer us all at first, an' will take some gittin' used to. Seems thet all of our energy should be goin' into makin' the adjustment of livin' one with the other."

He lifted her chin and looked into her eyes.

"You've got ya a big job, Marty. Already ya have yer hands full with yer own young'uns. Addin' two more ain't gonna lessen yer load none. I hope ya ain't takin' on too much. Yer tender heart may jest break yer back, I'm a thinkin'."

She shook her head.

"He answered our prayer, Clark. Iffen He thinks this right, what we're doin', then He'll give the strength thet we need too, won't He?"

Clark nodded. "I reckon He will," was all he said.

## Chapter 12

# *Nandry an' Clae*

True to his promise, Jedd arrived the next day with the two girls. Their few belongings were carried in a box and deposited in the bedroom that would be theirs. Marty wondered if the parting would be difficult for them, but there seemed to be no emotion shown by either side.

Jedd was anxious to be off. He had packed his possessions in his wagon, and with the money from the sale of the farm lying heavy in his pocket, he was hard-put to hold back, even for a cup of coffee. He did fill up on fresh bread and jam, however, and with the food barely swallowed announced that he must be on his way. He gave Marty and his two daughters a quick nod, which Marty supposed was to suffice for thank you, good-bye and God bless you, all three, and went out the door. He was full of the coming trip west and of all of the good fortune that he was sure it would hold. Jedd always had regarded good fortune more highly than hard work.

Thus it was that Nandry and Clae were established as members of the Davis household.

Marty decided to give the girls a few days of "settlin' in" before establishing routine and expectations.

She looked at their sorry wardrobe and decided that a trip to town would be necessary if they were to be suitably dressed for the soon-to-commence school classes.

Marty seldom went to town, sending instead a well-item-
ized list with Clark, but she felt that this time she should go
herself. Clark would find the selecting of dress materials and
other articles difficult and time consuming.

Marty had been saving egg-and-cream money over the
months and felt that now was the time to dip into her savings.
It wasn't fair to lay all of the expenses on Clark. He had already had to pay Jedd for the dubious privilege of raising his
daughters. Marty felt her hackles raise at the thought.

Well, that was all passed and done—so be it. From here on
they were hers to care for, and to the best of her ability, she
planned to do it right!

Nandry seemed her usual withdrawn self, neither expecting nor finding life to be interesting, but Clae seemed to observe everything around her and even dared at times to delight
in what she discovered.

Both girls were surprisingly helpful—a fact for which
Marty was grateful. Nandry preferred to spend time with
young Arnie rather than the other members of the family.
Marty did not mind, for help with the adventuresome and often mischievous little boy was always welcomed.

Marty planned her journey to town for the following Saturday. She would go in with Clark and thus save an extra trip.

On Friday after breakfast was over, she called the girls to
her. It was time, she decided, that they work a few things out.

They sat down silently, their hands nervously twisting in
their laps. Marty smiled at them in an effort to relieve their
tension.

"I thought thet it be time thet we have a chat," she began.

They did not move nor speak.

"Is yer room okay?"

Clae nodded and Nandry followed suit. The fact was that
Clae had never believed that anything so fine really existed.
The bed was soft with warm, nice-smelling blankets, colorful
rugs were scattered over the floor, printed curtains with ruffles
hung at the window and two framed pictures graced the wall.
A neat row of pegs was on the wall behind the door and a
wooden chest stood beneath the window. There was even a

small bench with cushions all of its own. How could she ask if the room was all right? Clae nodded mechanically, trying to keep the sparkle from bubbling up into her eyes.

Marty continued to smile.

"I thought maybe we should be sortin' out our work. Missie washes the dishes two mornin's a week, an' she cleans her room—makes her bed and hangs up her clothes each day—an' she helps some with Arnie, too. Now then, what ya be thinkin' thet you'd like to be doin' fer yer share-like?"

No response.

"I know thet ya already been makin' yer bed. Thet's good; an' ya do a nice job of it, too. But, is there enythin' thet ya 'specially like to do? Better than other things, I mean."

Still no answer.

Marty felt trapped, and just when she was wondering whether to assign the work as she saw fit, or to dismiss the two and forget the whole thing, assistance came to her from her own Missie.

"Mama says I wash dishes good," Missie announced, "but I'll share. Do ya want to wash dishes sometimes, Nandry?"

Nandry nodded.

"An' do you too, Clae?"

Clae nodded.

"Well," said Missie, very grown-up like, "then why don't we take turns?"

It was settled.

Missie went on. "We all need to make our own beds, but Clare is too little yet to make his bed, an' Arnie can't make a bed atall! Ya have to git 'im up an' dress 'im every day. Who wants to make Clare's bed an' who wants to dress Arnie?"

"I'll care fer Arnie," Nandry was quick to say.

"Then I'll make Clare's bed, I guess," spoke Clae.

"An' sometimes there's special jobs," went on Missie, "like gittin' more wood, or hangin' out clothes, or peelin' the vege'bles."

"I'd rather feed the chickens," Nandry said slowly. "An' gather eggs," she added as an afterthought.

"She likes chickens," Clae informed. "She was always

wishin' thet she had some. Chickens an' babies—thet's what she likes."

"Fine," said Marty, "you can feed the chickens and gather the eggs iffen ya like thet. What 'bout you, Clae? What would you be likin'?"

Clae looked suddenly shy. Dared she express her likes? Finally she blurted it out. She might have to pay for it, but say it she would.

"I'd like to learn to make things," she said, "pretty dresses an' aprons an' knitted things."

"Stop it, Clae," Nandry scolded. "Ya know thet ya can't do all thet. Ya'd wreck the machine fer sure."

Now it was out. Marty had noticed the young girl eying her machine hungrily. So she wished to be creative. Well, she would be given instruction and opportunity.

"The machine doesn't break so easy," she said, carefully choosing her words. "Ya must both learn to sew, an' then you'll be able to make whatever ya want. Perhaps we could start on somethin' simple, an' then when ya practice abit ya can do somethin' more fancy. I learned to sew when I was quite young, an' I've always been glad thet I did. Sewin' somethin' pretty always makes me feel good inside."

Clae's eyes shone. She could hardly believe her ears. Could she really learn to sew at this house? She wanted to hug this woman but she held back.

Marty went on.

"Now tomorra you are goin' to have yer first big job. I'm goin' into town with my husband to buy the things thet you'll be needin' fer school, an' I will be leavin' ya here on yer own."

Marty secretly wondered if she would be brave enough to leave them when the time came, or would she bundle them all up and take them along. No, that would never do. Five youngsters underfoot while she tried to hurry through a great deal of shopping just wouldn't work at all. Besides, the girls really did need the opportunity to prove themselves. They were quite old enough to be caring for younger ones, and she must give them the chance to show it.

Her announcement caused no change of expression in the

eyes that were before her.

"Do ya think, Nandry, thet ya can care fer young Arnie, an' help fix some dinner fer ya all?"

Nandry shook her head in agreement.

"An', Clae, you an' Missie will need to help with the dishes an' the dinner, an' keep an' eye on Clare. Can ya do thet?"

The two girls exchanged glances, then agreed.

"Good," said Marty, "then it be decided. Now we have lots thet must be done today. First I want ya all to slip off yer shoes so thet I can get a tracin' of yer feet fer new boots fer school."

Embarrassment flushed Marty's face as she realized too late that the two Larson girls were not wearing shoes.

"Our shoes are all worn out," Clae explained, matter-of-factly. "They won't stay on no more."

Marty carefully traced and labelled the feet on her pieces of cardboard. She would cut them out later so that they could be slipped into a shoe for fitting.

"Now then," she told the girls, "Clae an' Missie are to do up the dishes. Missie, you show Clae where the pans an' towels are kept. Nandry you come with me an' I'll show ya how to be carin' fer the chickens. Then we will gather an' clean the eggs so thet I can add 'em to the ones I've set aside to take to town."

"Can I bring Arnie?" Nandry asked. "He likes chickens, too."

Marty consented, knowing it to be true. Arnie did love the chickens, though Marty was convinced that what he liked the most was the delightful squawking and flapping they did when he chased them round the pen.

They left the house together. The two younger girls were already at work on the dishes.

Maybe things would fall into place after all. The girls all seemed almost eager to get to their new tasks. Marty breathed a relieved sigh and led the way to the grain bin.

## Chapter 13

# *The Trip to Town*

Marty still felt some misgivings on the following morning as she tied on her bonnet and gathered her eggs, butter and cream for her trip to town. Should she leave them all on their own or should she at least take Arnie with her? No. She must let the girls feel that she could trust them. After all, their father had made them shoulder grown-up responsibilities for years. She couldn't ask them to go back to being mere children again.

With reluctant steps she left to join Clark in the wagon. She waved good-bye again and put on a brave smile.

"Bring us some yummies," Clare called to her.

"An' some new hair ribbons fer school," added Missie.

"Thet girl," laughed Clark; "she thinks far too much 'bout how she be lookin'."

Marty coaxed forth a smile.

"Clark," she said as they left the gate, "do ya think it be okay to leave 'em like thet—with jest the girls an'—"

"Why not?" Clark interrupted. "They been cookin' an' cleanin' fer years already."

"But they haven't had young'uns to care fer."

"No, thet's right, but carin' fer young'uns seems to be the one thing thet pleasures young Nandry."

"I noticed thet, too," Marty responded. "She really seems

to enjoy Arnie. An' he seems to like her, too. Oh, I hope thet it will be all right, but I won't feel easy-like until we git home agin. I sure hope thet this is a fast trip."

"Yer frettin' too much I'm a thinkin', but we'll try to hurry it abit. Won't take me long to be a carin' fer the things thet I be needin'. How 'bout you?"

"Shouldn't take long. I need things fer the girls fer school an' the usual groceries."

"You be needin' money then."

"I have my egg savin's."

"No need to spend all yer savin's on outfittin' the girls. I'm willin' to share in the carin' of 'em."

Clark tucked the reins between his knees and pulled out his wallet. He extracted a couple of bills.

"Think this be enough?"

"Thet'll be fine," she answered. "I 'preciate it. It's gonna take abit to git 'em off to school proper-like. They really own nothin' now thet's fittin' to wear."

Clark nodded.

"Well, we knew when we took 'em thet they'd cost somethin'. No problem there."

They drove on in silence.

The town that day was filled with commotion. A wagon train was getting ready to move on. Dogs barked, horses stomped and children ran yelling through the street. Grown men argued prices and women scurried about, running to the store for a last-minute purchase or looking for children who had been told to stay put but didn't. Marty decided that she had picked a poor day to come to town; surely her shopping would be slowed down considerably.

She entered McDonald's General Store with some trepidation. She always dreaded facing this woman's scrutinizing eyes and equally sharp tongue.

"I declare," she had said to Clark on one occasion, "thet there woman's tongue has no sense of propriety."

Missie had overheard the word and loved it, and was henceforth declaring of all things—particularly to young Clare—"You've no sense of pa'piety," which seemed to be meaning "Yer jest plain dumb."

Marty had guarded her tongue more carefully in Missie's presence after that.

Marty now straightened her back and pushed herself through the McDonald's door. To her relief Mrs. McDonald was busy with three women from the train. She looked at Marty and her eyes held the expression of a child denied a cone at the annual Sunday school picnic. Marty smiled briefly and crossed to the bolts of dress goods. What relief to be left on her own for her choosing. Mentally she calculated as she lifted bolt after bolt. The new dresses had to be servicable, but, oh, how she'd like to have them pretty, too, and the prettier material added up so quickly. The dark blue would wear half of forever, but how would one ever make it look attractive. The soft pink voile was so beautiful but looked like you could sip tea through it without even changing the taste. Hardly the right thing for a farm girl.

Mrs. McDonald had reluctantly turned her full attention back to the ladies from the train and was now enjoying the bits of gossip that they could supply—prying rather unsubtlely for the whys of their coming or going. Marty went carefully about her choosing, weighing her decisions with care. She picked neither the dark blue nor the pink. "No use takin' material thet'll wear too long," she reasoned. "They'll outgrow it 'fore ya know it enyway." She took instead a length of medium blue, a pearly grey, some warm brown and a couple of prints, one with a green background and the other red. She then chose materials for underclothes, nighties, and bonnets and moved on to choose stockings, boots, and some heavier material for coats. Until the colder weather arrived the girls could get by with capes she would make out of material she already had on hand.

She realized as she added bolt to bolt on the counter, to later be measured off, what a mammoth sewing job she had ahead of her. She was thankful that she already had Missie's clothes prepared.

Missie! She had asked for new hair ribbons. Marty moved on to choose some. Nandry and Clae would need some too.

Her shopping was going well, thanks to the wagon-train ladies. She laid the last dry goods items with the pile on the
counter and rechecked her list. Even with the money that
Clark had given her, most of her egg-and-cream money would
go. Well, she couldn't help that. She had promised Tina Larson that she would give the girls a chance, and give them a
chance she would.

She went on to her grocery list, placing items on the
counter as she selected them. Before she had finished, Clark
entered the store. His eyebrows raised somewhat at the great
heap on the counter, but he made no comment.

"Most done," Marty offered. "Did ya git the things ya be
needin'?"

"All but a piece fer the plow. The smithie had to order thet
in, but I expected thet. Thet's why I sent now 'stead of waitin'
fer later." He grinned. "There be jest a chance thet it'll make
it fer spring plowin'."

The train ladies gathered their bundles and left the store,
and Mrs. McDonald scurried toward Clark and Marty as
though not to waste a precious minute of gossip time.

"Well, well, how are the Davises?" she began, but left no
time for a reply.

"I hear thet ya took on them two Larson girls." Her eyes
dared them to deny it and at the same instant declared them
out of their mind for so doing.

She waited just a moment but neither Clark nor Marty
commented.

"I have my purchases laid out here, Mrs. McDonald,"
Marty said evenly. "I believe thet's all I be a needin' today."

Mrs. McDonald went to work on adding up the groceries,
but her eyes promised Marty that she wasn't finished with her
yet. When she had the total figured, Clark stepped forward to
pay the bill.

"I'll take the groceries on out to the wagon," he informed
Marty, "then be back to help with them other things."

"I can manage 'em," Marty assured him. "Jest wait in the
wagon fer me. Where is the team?"

"Jest across the street."

"Fine. I'll be there quick-like."

Marty walked to the door with him and opened it as he went out, both arms loaded. She picked up the box she had left by the entrance, then placing it on the counter, she spoke to Mrs. McDonald.

"My eggs, butter, and cream fer today. I'd like 'em to go toward these things, please."

Mrs. McDonald began to calculate the exchange. When she had figured the worth of the farm produce, Marty began to push bolts of material forward, naming the yardage that she desired from each one. In between snips of the scissors, Mrs. McDonald managed to pry for tidbits that she might later be able to pass on.

"Jedd said ya was most keen on keepin' the girls."

Marty only nodded.

"People here figurin' as to why. Some say thet with yer own three young'uns ya figured to need the help pretty bad. I said, 'Now, Mrs. Davis wouldn't stoop to usin' child labor like,' but—" She stopped and shrugged her shoulders to indicate that she could be wrong.

" 'Seemed to me thet it makes more sense to keep 'em fer their board,' seys I. 'Girls thet age ain't much fer workin', but with Jedd a jinglin' all thet hard cash no reason thet the Davises shouldn't git in on some of it.' "

Marty could feel her cheeks flushing with anger. How this woman could goad her.

"Enyway, I says to folks thet, knowin' ya like, I'm right sure thet Miz Davis won't overwork those two, an' a bit of good hard work might be the best thing fer 'em. Never did care much fer those two—real shifty eyes. Grow up useless like their pa. I'll bet ya won't git much work outta those two, but iffen ya got a fair cash exchange—"

Marty could take no more.

"Mrs. McDonald," she said, trying hard not to let her anger show through her words, though she knew that she wasn't succeeding, "we took the girls 'cause their ma wanted 'em to have a chance, an' I made a promise-like 'fore she died. I aim to keep thet promise iffen I can—an' there was no money,

Mrs. McDonald. Fact is, my husband had to pay Jedd Larson to be 'llowed to keep his daughters.''

"I see . . ." Mrs. McDonald's eyes said smugly. "Thet's what I wanted to know. Why didn't ya say so without all the fuss? Some people were so close-like with information.''

Then she added, "Thet's jest what I been a figurin'. Thought me thet folks were wrong in their sayin'.''

Mrs. McDonald had scored again. Why does she always get what she wants from me? Marty fumed. She had told no one else of her promise to Tina except Ma, and Ma guarded secrets carefully. Now the whole county would know, and it would change as it was passed from mouth to mouth.

She fought for her composure, paid for the purchases and gathered her parcels. They made quite a load and she wished that she had accepted Clark's offer to return to help her.

"All them fancy things ain't fer those girls, are they? Seems to me thet stuck way out there on yer farm, ya could jest as leave patch up their old things.''

"The girls will be goin' to school come September." Marty said the words firmly. There was just a trace of pride in her voice. Before Mrs. McDonald could say anything further, Marty headed for the door with quick, firm steps.

As she entered the street the commotion from the wagon train was even more intense. The teams were lined up now, ready to leave within a few minutes. Horses still stomped, dogs still barked, and children still yelled, but the bartering of the men was over and the last-minute purchases of the women had been made. People stood in clusters by the wagons saying farewells and giving last-minute messages to be passed on to someone at the other end of the journey.

The third wagon back must be a passenger wagon, Marty decided, for miscellaneous and sundry people seemed to be aboard it. The canvas, for the present, was down and several plank seats had been placed across the wagon box. Most of the passengers appeared to be making a journey of short duration, perhaps to a nearby larger center, for they travelled light. They appeared to be men on business or women going out to shop or visit. Some of them had young family members with them, whose faces showed anticipation at the prospect of the trip.

In the midst of the clamor and excitement sat a white-faced somber-eyed lady with three small children. One child cried, another clung to his mother fearfully, and the third and oldest sat hollow-cheeked and drawn apart.

"Thet's Miz Talbot from the other side of town," said a voice at Marty's shoulder, and she turned slightly to see that Mrs. McDonald had come from the store to get in on all of the activity.

"Never should 'ave come west," she stated; "not made of the right stuff. She's leavin'. Goin' back."

Her words were clipped and biting. Marty looked at the poor girl and wished with all of her heart that she had had a chance to speak with her.

Suddenly through the crowd a young man came pushing, almost at a run. The oldest child jumped to his feet, arms open wide, and squealed with delight. The woman looked alarmed. Marty could not hear the words, but she sensed that the man was arguing and pleading for the woman to stay, but she set her lips tightly and shook her head. Finally she turned her back on him completely, her shoulders held stiff and stubborn.

The order of "move out" was given, and with a creak and a grind the cumbersome wagons began to move forward. The man had to disentangle himself from the arms of the crying child and gently push him back into the wagon. The child screamed and shouted after him, and Marty thought for one terrifying moment that he was going to jump.

"All his life he'll wish he had left those two little arms around his neck and kept thet young boy with him," Marty thought.

The wagon moved on past her. She could not see the woman's face, but she noticed that her shoulders had lost their defiance and were now shaking convulsively.

"Oh, you stubborn thing," Marty's heart cried; "go back—go back," but the wagon moved on.

Marty turned to see the man, hands over his face, leaning

against a hitching rail for support, the sobs wrenching his whole body.

A sickness filled her whole being. It was wrong, it was wicked, it was so cruel to tear a family apart like that.

"Good riddance, seys I," said the voice beside her, and Marty turned quickly away and stumbled across the street to the waiting wagon.

Clark placed her bundles in the wagon box and helped her up. Then the team, at his command, moved out of town.

They had gone some distance in silence, the warm summer sun shining down upon late flowers waving at the sides of the road, birds dipping back and forth in the path of the team. Marty's anger and hurt had somewhat subsided, but her confused thoughts still fought to sort it all out.

Suddenly she felt her hand gripped tightly and looked up into Clark's probing eyes.

"So ya saw it too, huh?" he questioned.

She shook her head dumbly, her eyes filling with tears.

He squeezed her hand.

"Oh, Clark," she said when she finally felt controlled enough to speak. "It was so wrong, so awful, an'—an'—it could have been *me*," she finished lamely.

"But it wasn't," he answered firmly; "it wasn't, an'—somehow—somehow, I really don't think thet it ever could've been."

Marty looked up in surprise to meet his even gaze. Their unspoken communication somehow assured her.

"No," she finally said with conviction, "no, maybe it never could've."

Clark was right for her—so right. Their love was strong and good. The good Lord had so prepared them for each other—even when Marty didn't know Him, and had loathed the thought of staying on with Clark. Yes, their love had promise—enduring promise.

# Chapter 14

## *The Family*

Marty's next few weeks were busy ones. Besides the usual daily chores and caring for the garden, she had the sewing to do for the Larson girls. Nandry seemed to accept the new things as unconsequential, but Clae's eyes took on a shine. Marty found herself instructing the young girl in the art of sewing and discovered her to be a good student. This pleased them both and Clae was encouraged to do more and more. Nandry also was shown how to sew, but though she went through the motions, and did well enough at it, she never seemed to be too enthused. She was much more interested in caring for Arnie and entertaining Clare. Nandry's contribution to the household was much appreciated. With the two small boys out from underfoot, Marty's and Clae's sewing progressed without interruption, as did the other tasks that needed to be done.

Clark looked at the finished garments and smiled his approval. *His* girls would all look "jest fine a-sittin' in thet new schoolroom," he declared. Nandry flushed and Clae beamed at being included as his girls.

Marty began to notice little things concerning Nandry and wondered if indeed the young girl maybe "overcared" for her benefactor. Clark's appearance was the only thing that ever brought a change of expression to Nandry's face, and Marty often caught her watching Clark as he went about the yard. She noticed as Nandry set the table that Clark's plate and cutlery were arranged with special care.

"I think thet I'll be plum glad to git thet girl off to school," she told herself one day and immediately reprimanded herself.

"Ya silly young goose," she scolded, coloring in spite of herself. "Here ya are havin' jealous pangs over a mere child."

It surprised her somewhat to discover her jealousy. She had never been in a situation to feel threatened before, never having had to share Clark with anyone but her children.

"God, fergive me," she prayed, "an' help me not to be selfish with the man I love. Nandry is growin' up, perhaps too quickly, but it be by no choice of her own. She didn't have much to look up to in her own pa, an' now seein' a man, thoughtful an' carin', hardworkin' an' with humor in his eyes, no wonder she admires 'im like. Enyway, Lord, help me to be wise an' to be just. Help me to love Nandry an' to help her through these painful years of growin' up. Help Clark, too. Give 'im wisdom in his carin'."

Marty made no mention of her observations to Clark. There was no use drawing his attention to something of which he seemed to be completely unaware. It could accomplish no good, and perhaps would only serve to put an unnatural restraint between the man and the girl, and Nandry so much needed to be able to reach out to people. Secretly, Marty hoped that Clark would never realize that the young girl was nursing a "crush."

For the most part Clark was away in the fields, and though Nandry cared for the chickens and the little ones in comparative silence, Marty still observed the looking-off in the direction that Clark was working, and the flush of the cheeks when he entered the house. Clark never did seem to notice and teased each of *his girls* equally.

Missie was still number one and being only "goin' on six" could still climb on her pa's knee, insist on combing his hair, or curl up beside him under the shelter of his arm.

Clare was his "helper" and followed his father wherever his young steps were able. It often meant a piggyback return, for the young Clare played out quickly.

Arnie's tottering steps determined to follow Pa also, and

Marty, looking out of the window, often shook her head at the patient Clark trying to chore with two small boys assisting him, making his tasks most difficult, yet enjoyable.

Though patient and loving with his family, Clark was very firm, and Marty at times had to bite her tongue when she felt that Clark was expecting a bit much for their tender years. She would have coddled them, Clark would not, for he had a strong conviction that what was learned through discipline in early years would not have to be learned through more painful lessons later on.

Clae seemed almost to forget that she had ever lived elsewhere but with the Davises; and though she did not call Clark and Marty Pa and Ma, Marty felt that she truly looked on them as such. She openly admired Clark and enjoyed his teasing, even teasing back in return, her eyes sparkling with amusement.

So they adjusted to one another and began to feel as a family. Morning worship was a special time. The two oldest girls listened carefully to things that they had never heard before, while Missie and Clare coaxed for their favorite Bible stories.

The days passed quickly. Enough of the sewing was done so that the girls at least could start school dressed appropriately. Marty would finish the rest as she found the time.

Missie's excitement grew. Marty felt that she was on the verge of hysteria and tried to slow her down. Clark just laughed and said to let her enjoy it. Daily, Missie changed her mind about what she would wear on her first day, going from plaid, to grey, to blue, to plaid again—over and over. Finally she settled on the blue because she liked her blue hair ribbons the best. Her only sorrow was that Tommie would not be there.

"I'm gonna marry Tommie," she informed Clae.

"Yer only five," Clae responded.

"Almost six, an' I'll grow," Missie retorted.

"But Tommie's most twenty."

"So!" said Missie, and that settled it.

Marty felt that it would indeed be good for Missie to have more contact with other children. She'd be right glad when school was finally in session.

# Chapter 15

# *The New Teacher*

The Saturday before school was to begin was a special day for the whole community. A meeting was called at the school-house for all interested parties. It was a chance for the parents and children to meet Mr. Wilbur Whittle, and vice versa. Marty supposed that there wasn't a home in the whole area that wasn't touched by the excitement.

The meeting was scheduled for two o'clock and the ladies had decided to serve coffee and cake at its closing. "Eatin' together always breaks the ice, so to speak," observed Mrs. Stern, who still had youngsters young enough to be sent to school.

At the Davis house the noon meal was hurried through and the dishes quickly done. Careful attention was then given to the grooming of each family member. Nandry and Clae had never looked better. Nandry still looked noncommittal, though Marty did see her glance at Clark for his appraisal. Clae, on the other hand, primped and preened. She was not unattractive and with her eyes shining and her cheeks flushed, she looked downright pretty. The fact that Clae had helped to sew the dress she wore filled her with pride. Marty sensed it and complimented her, making her rosy cheeks turn even rosier. Marty commented on Nandry's appearance as well. Nandry's eyes lit momentarily but she didn't allow herself a smile.

Missie pranced around the house, excitement oozing out of every pore. She had Clare and little Arnie doing somersaults and jigs with her. Finally Clark and Marty were able to usher their brood out the door in some semblance of order.

It was a beautiful day for a meeting of neighbors and everyone seemed to turn out. The teams were tied at the far end of the lot and the folk gathered next to the schoolhouse, there not being enough room for them all to go inside.

Neighbor greeted neighbor, with good-natured talk flowing all around. The two spring babies were there. Little Elizabeth Anne was radiant with smiles and coos. She insisted on being held upright so that she wouldn't miss a thing, and even tried to sit on her own. A "bundle of wigglin' energy," her proud Grandma called her. Marty took a turn holding her and had to agree with the verdict.

Wanda and Cam were there with their new son. Everett Cameron DeWinton John—Marty thought it a big name for a small boy and was somewhat surprised to learn that his father had cut it down to plain "Rett." Rett had gained rapidly. He was already a big boy for his age, having quickly compensated for his size at birth.

"Look at thet, huh," his father boasted. "Look at thet fer a boy, an' 'im not yet five months. Gonna be a big fella thet 'un." He grinned broadly.

Marty agreed and took the baby. She held Rett for some time and finally had to acknowledge the little warning signals that shivered up her arms and to her heart. The baby did not move as a youngster should. When she raised him to her shoulder there wasn't the proper lift of his head. Something was wrong with this baby. She looked at his beaming mother, his boasting pa, and prayed that her eyes wouldn't betray her, that she would be proved wrong; but she could not shake the heavy feeling from her heart.

At ten past two the Watley wagon finally pulled in, bringing with them the new teacher. All eyes were on this man. Marty wasn't sure what any of them had expected, but she was willing to bet that none of them had pictured him as he was. Accustomed to seeing big, muscular men on the frontier, this one looked terribly out of place. Not only was he short, but very small of build and bone, and his sleeve size did not seem to have to expand one bit for his biceps from that which covered the slim wrist. What he lacked in size he seemed to endeavor to compensate with mustache. Though carefully tended and waxed on the ends, the furry appendage nearly hid the lower half of his face and stuck out beyond his face like handles on a walking plow.

His vest was a bright plaid material and he wore white spats. A bowler hat topped his small cocky head, and he spent a good deal of his time reaching for it, dusting it and then replacing it again.

Marty noted his eyes with approval. They looked both intelligent and just a trifle humorous.

Clark was to chair the meeting and he gave his welcome to Mr. Wilbur Whittle in a most courteous fashion. The people responded with applause. Clark then introduced the neighborhood families, having them stand together so that each family could be properly introduced and recognized. Mr. Whittle nodded at each one, but remained silent.

After all had been presented, the new teacher was given the floor. Marty expected to hear a small voice that would suit the small man, but was surprised when a deep bass voice emerged.

"Why, he musta practiced fer years to be able to do thet," she thought.

In spite of the deepness, Mr. Whittle's voice was not loud, and those listening had to strain to hear his words.

He expressed his pleasure at being selected to be the instructor in their school.

"Ya were all we could git," thought Marty.

He was charmed with the fine boarding place they had so thoughtfully provided.

"An' she was the only one with room," Marty admitted.

He was gratified to behold the fine facilities and careful selection of instructional aids.

Marty wasn't sure just what he was referring to, so let that pass.

He was looking forward to an amicable relationship with each one in the community, adult and child alike. He would look forward to further acquaintance, for he knew that it would be both stimulating and intellectually rewarding.

Classes would begin on the Monday next at nine o'clock sharp, the bell employed at five minutes of the hour. Each child was to be seated and ready to commence the opening exercises on the hour. No tardiness would be accepted. Two breaks of fifteen minutes each would be given during the day, and an hour at midday to allow for the partaking of the noon meal and a time of physical stimulation for the students. Classes would end at three o'clock p.m. each day.

The children would get the benefit of his undivided attention and unsurpassed education, he having been trained in one of the country's foremost institutions, recognized universally for its top-quality professors and its comprehensive and exhaustive courses.

He continued on for a few minutes more, but Marty's attention was diverted by Mrs. Vickers who leaned toward Mrs. Stern and whispered, rather loudly, "I hope he means he still 'tends to teach."

Mrs. Stern assured her that he did.

The meeting finally ended with the community crowd giving the teacher a loud round of applause, and he beaming on the group, withdrew, doffing his bowler hat.

Coffee and cake were served and visiting with the neighbors resumed. Clark sought out Marty to meet the new neighbors on the Larson place. She was happy to do so and excused herself from the ladies with whom she had been chatting.

The LaHayes seemed a nice couple. Mrs. LaHaye still looked thin and drawn but assured Marty that she was feeling much better and was sure that she'd soon be on her feet again. Arrangements were made for the LaHayes to join the Davises for Sunday dinner.

Mr. LaHaye was disappointed that his journey west was cut short of purpose, but was farmer enough to see the possibility of Jedd Larson's good farmland. He had plans for replacing the farmhouse and buildings, which had already undergone some much-needed repairs.

Tessie, their only girl, was plain but pleasant. Marty took to her immediately. Nathan, the older boy, was rather outspoken for a boy of his age. He appeared to feel snugly confident about his own wit and ability. The younger boy, Willie, had a sparkle in his brown eyes that endeared him to Marty, and at the same time warned her. No telling what this youngster would think to try.

"How old are ya, Willie?" Marty asked.

"Nine," he responded, good-naturedly. "I been in school before. Took three grades already."

Marty was wondering if he was thinking that that put him in a class by himself, for it was a well-known fact that none of the children in the area had as yet had any formal education.

"Guess ya'll be able to help the kids here quite a bit then," Marty said and watched carefully for Willie's reaction.

"Some of 'em," he said carelessly. "If I want to. Some—" he hesitated. "I might help her," he said with a grin, pointing a finger.

Marty followed the pointed index finger and noted with a bit of alarm that the "her" on the other end was none other than Missie.

"Don't expect she'll need more help than the teacher can give," she said. "She's just startin' first grade, an' she already knows her letters and numbers."

Willie shrugged again and continued to grin. "Might help her enyway," he said; then he was off on a run to rejoin the other children.

Marty turned back to the adult conversation at hand. The LaHayes were leaving early. He had much to do. Shouldn't really have taken the time off, but his wife fussed about gettin' the boys in school. Well, they'd better git on home. He had a pasture to fence to supply his cattle with better grazin'. Glad to make acquaintance. They'd look forward to Sunday dinner—and they were gone.

# Chapter 16

## *School Begins*

Monday morning, instead of being bright and sunny as had been ordered, dawned overcast and showery. Missie despaired as she looked out of the window.

"My new blue dress will get all wet," she wailed. "An' so will my brand new hair ribbons."

Clark came to the rescue by offering to hitch up the team to drive the girls to school. This idea met with unanimous approval, and Missie's cheerful disposition returned even if the sun did not shine.

Marty carefully packed lunches and supervised the combing of hair and cleaning of fingernails. She didn't know who felt the most excitement, but was almost sure that it was a close race between Missie and herself.

Clark decided that Clare and Arnie should go along for the ride in spite of the drizzly day.

"They won't melt," he said, "an' it will be good fer 'em to feel a part of the action."

The breakfast prayer that morning included the three new scholars—that they would study well, show their teacher due respect, and use what they would learn for the bettering of self and all mankind.

After the meal was over the excited group left the house, and Clark bundled the girls in the wagon to keep the rain off their new clothes. Clare and Arnie, feeling proud and important, took their places beside Clark on the wagon seat. Marty felt a thickness in her throat as she watched the eager faces, taking particular note of Missie's shining eyes. And they were off.

"First school, then marriage, an' gone fer good," she said softly. " 'Fore we know it, they'll all be gone—one by one."

She brushed the tears from her eyes and turned back to the dishes. Soon Clark would return with Clare and Arnie, and all the work of their care and entertainment would fall on her now that the girls were away. She must hurry through her morning tasks in order to be ready to spend much of this rainy day amusing two restless little boys.

The boys returned and Clark brought them in. Marty changed them into dry clothes and made suggestions as to what they might like to do. She had thought herself prepared for what was in store but found that it was even worse than what she had imagined.

Arnie fussed and refused to be pacified with toys. Clare insisted that he should be able to go to school, too. When Marty failed to be convinced, he plagued her to let him go out to play. She pointed out the window at the crying sky, but Clare only whined and seemed to imply that Marty could do something about the weather if she would just put her mind to it.

Marty gave them each a cookie. Arnie shared his with Miss Puss and immediately undid all of his kindness by deliberately pulling the kitten's tail. She responded by scratching his hand. Arnie's howl brought Clare on the run. He chased the cat behind the kitchen stove and proceeded to poke at her with the broom handle. Marty sent Clare to sit on a chair and washed and cared for the scratches on Arnie's hand.

By mid-morning the clouds cleared away and the sun returned. Marty was glad to give in to Clare's coaxing to go outside. She was afraid that he would stay out only long enough to get thoroughly wet, but even that would give her some measure of respite.

As she suspected, the puddles drew Clare like a magnet, but he played in them only long enough to become wet and muddy and then returned to the door complaining that there was nothing to do. Marty despaired as she cleaned him up. What would she ever do with them through this long, long day?

Noon finally arrived and Clark came in for lunch. The boys squealed with delight and Marty heaved a sigh of relief. At least here was a little release, and after the meal she could tuck them in for a nap.

But the nap-time didn't go well either. Arnie fussed and fretted—unusual for him—and Clare never did go to sleep.

The seemingly endless day finally righted itself when the three girls came home. Arnie ran to Nandry with a glad cry, and Clare began questioning Missie to see if she had really learned anything. Clae stood by smiling demurely as though she had some great secret.

Marty had to force herself into the circle to be seen and heard.

"How'd it go?"

"Oh, Mama," cried Missie, "it's jest so great! Guess what I learned—jest guess. Here I'll show ya."

"I want to see," said Marty, "an' I can hardly wait, but first how 'bout ya all change yer school dresses an' hang 'em up nice."

The girls went to comply.

The time following was spent telling of the day's many activities. Only Nandry had nothing to say. Missie babbled on and on about the teacher, the other kids, the new work, her desk, and the poor fire in the pot-bellied stove.

"Know what? I don't think Mr. Whittle ever built a fire afore. From now on Silas Stern is gonna build it. It smoked awful."

"I like Mary Lou Coffins. She's my favorite friend—'cept fer Faith Graham."

The Coffins were new to the area.

Missie continued, a twinkle in her eye.

"Guess what?" she said in a whisper. "Nathan LaHaye likes Clae."

Clae blushed and protested.

"He does too," declared Missie; "he pulled her braids an' everythin'."

Marty had no idea what the everythin' might be.

Then Missie's eyes took on fire. "But I hate thet Willie LaHaye. He's a show-off."

"Missie—shame on ya," admonished Marty. "We are not to hate anyone."

"Bet God didn't know 'bout Willie LaHaye when He made thet rule," Missie declared with venom. "*Nobody* could love him."

"What did he do thet was so terrible?"

"He reads—he reads real loud—he reads everythin'—even the eighth primer. He thinks he's smart. An' he teases too. He said thet I'm too cute to be dumb. He said he'd help me. I said, 'No, you won't,' an' he jest laughed an' said, 'Wait an' see.' Boy, he thinks he's smart. I wish my Tommie were there."

Missie tossed her head in such a fashion that Marty wondered where her little girl had so suddenly gone, to be replaced by this arrogant creature who deemed herself a young lady.

"Please," thought Marty, "don't let school change her thet much—thet fast," but the next moment the little girl was back again.

"Can I lick thet dish, Mama? I got so hungry today, an' guess what, Mama? Mary Lou has a shiny red pail to carry her lunch in. Could I have one too, Mama? It has a handle on it to carry it by and the letters on it are white."

"What kinda pail is it?"

"I don't know yet. I don't know the words, but it's so pretty, isn't it, Clae?"

Clae agreed that it was.

"Could I git one, Mama, please?" coaxed Missie.

"I don't know dear; we'll have to see." Marty was noncommittal.

"I don't like carryin' my lunch in thet old thing," pouted Missie. "Mary Lou's is lots nicer."

"We'll see," was as far as Marty would go.

The subject of school was dropped for the moment, but Missie picked it up again after supper when she had her father's attention.

"An' Mary Lou has a shiny red pail fer her lunch—with white letters an' a handle. Could I have one too, Pa, please?"

"Are shiny red lunch pails necessary fer learnin'?" Clark asked.

"Not fer learnin'—fer lookin' nice," Missie said with determination.

At least she's honest, thought Marty.

"We'll see," said her pa.

"Thet's what Mama said," Missie objected.

"Ya have a wise Mama," Clark told her, not at all moved by her cajoling.

Missie wrinkled her nose but said no more. She knew when she had reached her limit. She'd let the matter drop for the present.

# Chapter 17

## *School Days*

The days fell into a routine. Gradually the two boys accepted the fact of the girls' absence and adjusted their play to include one another.

The girls settled into a pattern of learning. Missie was quick and eager and was soon leading her class even without the help of Willie LaHaye. Clae, too, had taken to school and surprised and delighted both the teacher and the Davises with her ability. She loved books and would have spent all of her time buried in them had she been allowed to do so. Only Nandry seemed to drag her feet at the thought each morning of another day spent in school. Marty noticed it and wished that there was some way that she could help the girl. She knew that most of the beginners in the school were much younger than Nandry and that this in itself would be a discouragement to her. Marty endeavored to encourage without prodding.

Missie was the one who furnished the household with news of school. One day she came home giggling and even Clae joined in.

"Guess what? When Mr. Whittle goes to yell loud, his voice goes from way deep to a funny squeak." Missie demonstrated. Marty tried hard to retain the proper parental attitude of teacher respect. "The big boys like to make 'im yell so thet it happens. It sounds so funny, Mama, an' then he gits real red-like an' growls real low—like this." Missie growled as well as a six-year-old girl could.

"So," thought Marty, "he did cultivate his low voice, and doesn't always have it under control."

"I hope thet ya don't laugh at yer teacher," she said solemnly.

Missie hung her head, but when she raised it her eyes sparkled.

"Bet you'd laugh," she said, and hurried on, "but I jest laughed a little bit."

Missie also had frequent reports on "thet Willie LaHaye."

Willie LaHaye had dipped her hair ribbon in an ink-well.

Willie LaHaye had chased her with a dead mouse.

Willie LaHaye had put a grasshopper in her lunch box.

An' Willie LaHaye had carved her initials with his on a tree by the crik an' she'd scratched 'em out.

An' furthermore, she hated thet Willie LaHaye, an' she bet thet God didn't even care.

Thet dumb ole Willie LaHaye.

# Chapter 18

# *Somethin' New*

Clark made his usual trip to town on Saturday. Marty was glad that there was no good reason for her to go along. She might have enjoyed the break, being sure now that the girls were quite capable of caring for things while she was gone, if it hadn't been that to go to town meant facing Mrs. McDonald. The woman never failed to get Marty in an emotional corner. Marty declared that she'd rather face a bear or an Indian.

Indeed, Marty had faced very few Indians since she had come west and those that she had seen seemed harmless enough. Most of the Indians in their area had been moved on into the hill country and settled on a reserve set apart for them. Some wondered how they ever managed to survive there, but most contented themselves with the fact that an Indian was an Indian, and meant to survive on very little. In general the feeling of the settlers was "live and let live." As long as the Indian was no threat to their well-being, they were content to let him ride the hills hunting for his meat and tanning necessary hides. On the other hand, they felt no responsibility for, or obligation to, the welfare of the Indian.

As for the bear—Marty was glad that she had never had reason to concern herself with one of those either. Like the Indian, they were content to remain in their native hills, away from the smell and the guns of the settlers. Occasionally a neighbor lad felt that he must venture into the hills and return with a bearskin to place on the cabin floor or hang above the fireplace. This was a prestige symbol rather than a necessity.

Still, even when gazing at the huge fur hide with the head still carrying the fierce beady eyes and the long yellow teeth, Marty felt that either the bear or the Indian must be preferable to Mrs. McDonald, so Marty avoided town, somewhat ashamed of herself for doing so, yet content in her weakness.

The day passed quickly. Marty always looked forward to Saturdays. It gave her a chance to catch up on many odd jobs because the girls kept the little boys out from under her feet.

Tomorrow would be a special Sunday. The new schoolteacher would be coming to share the Sunday dinner with them. Marty both anticipated and dreaded it. What was this odd-looking man really like? Missie brought home both good and evil reports—one moment praising him, the next condemning his strange conduct, and the next breaking into uncontrollable giggles over his silly deportment.

Marty had set aside her freshly baked pies and was carefully cleaning two young roosters when Clark arrived.

As usual, his return brought the children running to meet him. Marty, watching from the window, saw Clark climb slowly and carefully down from the wagon. At first Marty felt a concern pass swiftly through her, wondering if Clark had somehow been injured, but he walked spryly as he headed for the house, the youngsters in tow. Marty noticed then that he carried something inside his jacket—there was a bulge there and he seemed to be carefully guarding it as he walked. The children had spied the bump, too, and their curiosity was as intense as Marty's, but Clark just grinned and motioned them on to the house.

"Now, what he be up to?" mused Marty, as she watched the little cavalcade draw nearer. Soon they were all inside, the children clamoring:

"What is it, Pa?"

"Whatcha got, huh?"

"Show us, Pa!"

Clark pulled back his jacket and a tawny, curly head

poked out. Sharp little eyes blinked at the sudden light, and the commotion about him brought a glad wiggle to the little body. Shrieks filled the air and each of the children pleaded to be the first to hold him.

"We start with the littlest first," said Clark, handing the squirming bundle to Arnie. Arnie giggled as he held the puppy close. It was the first time that Arnie had ever had a face-wash from a puppy's warm tongue. His eyes sparkled.

"Little boys and puppies belong together," thought Marty. Arnie must have thought so, too, for he was most reluctant to pass the puppy on to Clare.

As the children enthused over the new pup, Marty found opportunity to speak to Clark.

"Where'd ya git 'im?"

"The smithie's dog had a litter. Jest big enough now to wean. This one looks like the pick o' the pack to me."

"Sure a cutie."

"Yeah, an' look at the eyes—the head—looks like a smart 'un."

The children had finally agreed to put the puppy down so that they could watch it waddle and prance across the kitchen floor.

"Look at 'im! Look at 'im!" they cried, giggling and clapping at his silly antics.

"Well," said Clark, "let's take 'im out an' see what Ole Bob thinks of 'im."

Ole Bob was truly becoming *old* Bob. His legs were stiff and unaccommodating. His eyes were getting dim, and his movements slow. Clark and Marty had realized that Bob's days were numbered, but perhaps with care, he could be with them for several months yet.

The family followed Clare, who was carrying the puppy out to the doghouse where Ole Bob resided. Bob came out slowly, stretching his stiff muscles, and wagged a greeting to them all.

As the puppy was placed on the ground, Bob lowered his head slowly and sniffed. He didn't seem impressed, but he wasn't angered either. The puppy, upon being presented to one of his kind, went wild with excitement, bouncing and bobbing around on his unsteady feet like a funny wind-up toy whose spring would not run down. Ole Bob put up with his ridiculous display for a few moments, then walked away and lay down. The puppy toddled after him and began to tug at and wrestle his long fluffy tail. Bob chose to ignore him, as the children shrieked.

Eventually the puppy was left with Ole Bob. Clark and the boys went to put away the team and unload the wagon. The girls, after filling the puppy's little tummy with warm milk, returned to the chores they had been assigned. Each one had been advised to consider a name for the new dog. This would be discussed and settled at the supper table.

Marty went in to finish washing the chickens and clean the cupboard top, so that Clark and the boys could place the groceries there for her to put away.

As she went through the bags and boxes, she suddenly stopped short.

"What's this?" she asked, for the pails were clearly marked LARD. "I didn't have me lard on my list, did I? I got lard stacked up high from our last butcherin'."

Marty picked up her list and glanced over it to see what she might have ordered that Clark had read as lard.

"No," he answered evenly, "ya didn't have lard on the list."

"Then why—?" Marty left the question hanging. Clark looked a mite sheepish.

"They're red, ain't they—an' shiny—an' they have a handle—an' white letters?"

It finally dawned. Missie's pail. Red and shiny with white letters—LARD.

Marty nodded.

"Now, I ain't sayin' thet Missie should have thet jest cause she asked fer it." Clark hurried on. "No reason fer her to be thinkin' thet she'll always git what she's a wantin' jest by askin', but iffen ya think thet it won't hurt none, fer her to have it—like this once, then it'll be there. An'—well, I could hardly git her one an' not the other two—now could I?"

"No, I s'pose not."

Clark turned to leave the kitchen.

"Ya can decide," he said again.

Marty turned back to the three red, shiny pails. Three pails of lard, and she already with more lard than they could use, and another fall butchering coming up soon. What would she ever do with it all?

"Ya ole softy," she murmured, but she was forced to swallow hard, and the thought of the happy faces and Missie's glowing eyes when she passed them their lunches on Monday morning made it difficult to wait.

The chores had been done and the Saturday night bathwater put on the stove to heat in the big copper boiler, when the family gathered around for the evening meal.

"I thought thet iffen somethin' happens to Ole Bob, it'll make it less painful-like iffen they have a new pup to fill their minds," Clark confided in Marty as she dished up the potatoes. She nodded.

Clark moved on to the table and saw to the seating of his family.

"Know what, Ma?" said Clare. "I stopped to see the puppy an' it's all curled up sleepin' with Ole Bob. Does Ole Bob think he's the puppy's mama?"

Marty smiled. "No, I doubt Ole Bob be thet dumb, but as long as the puppy doesn't torment 'im too much a chewin' an' a chasin', Ole Bob'll be content to let 'im share his bed."

"He's so cute," said Missie. "I wish I could share my bed."

"Oh, no," said Marty firmly. "Animals belong outside, not in."

Thinking of Miss Puss, who did sneak in and share her bed, Missie did not belabor the point.

"Well," said Clark, "thought ya of any good names yet?"

"I think we should call 'im Cougar," said Clare.

"Cougar, fer a dog?" Missie was unimpressed.

"Thet's the color he is," argued Clare.

"I like King or Prince, or somethin' like thet," said Missie.

"Fer a little puppy?" Clare was just as incredulous.

"He'll grow," Missie said defiantly.

"What about you, Sport?" Clark asked Arnie. Arnie pushed in a big spoonful of potatoes and gravy with the help of his free hand. He shifted them around, swallowed some and then answered.

"Ole Bob."

"But what ya want to call the new puppy?"

"Ole Bob."

"But Ole Bob be the name of—Ole Bob," Clark finished lamely.

"I know," said Arnie. "I like it."

"Ya want Ole Bob an' Ole Bob?" asked Clare, thinking that only he was really capable of understanding and interpreting the young Arnie.

"Yeah," said Arnie shaking his head. "Now we got—" two rather potatoey fingers struggled to stand upright with the rest remaining tucked in. "Now we got two Ole Bobs."

The others all laughed, but it was finally agreed that the new puppy would carry the name of Ole Bob as well.

"He'll grow," said Missie.

"Yeah, an' he'll git old someday too," said Clare. " 'Sides when we call 'em, we'll jest hafta say one name an' they'll both come."

Clark smiled, "Save ourselves a heap of time and trouble thet way, won't we?"

Arnie grinned. "Now we got a little Ole Bob, an' a big Ole Bob."

As it happened, big Ole Bob did not stay with them for long. As Clark had hoped, the loss of the old dog was much easier for the children to accept with the growing young pup running and nipping at their heels.

## Chapter 19

# *Tommie's Friend*

The school year passed by quickly, and before it seemed possible it was time for the summer break. Some of the older boys left school early in order to help with the spring planting. Others carried on until the month of June. Missie ended her year by bringing home bouquets of flowers or red ripe strawberries in the red pail that had, over the winter months, lost a little of its shine.

Summer passed as quickly as it came—before, it seemed, they had time to enjoy it to its fullest.

Then it was fall again with the flurry of school preparations. Clare was still a year short of school age and again grumbled about being kept at home.

Clae and Missie were anxious to return. Clae had spent the summer poring over books that Mr. Whittle had supplied and was closing the gap between where she was and where she should have been with surprising speed. Mr. Whittle was pleased.

Missie, too, was a promising pupil and looked forward to school with much anticipation.

Only Nandry balked. At first she seemed just unenthused, but as the day for school opening drew nearer she finally dared voice her position.

"I'm not goin' back," she declared with finality, "—not with all those little kids."

She was so determined about it that Clark and Marty discussed it and decided that as much as they hated to do so, they would allow her to drop out.

"We'll jest have to concentrate on the homemaking an' the baby carin'," said Marty. "Nandry has the makin's of a good wife an' mother. Maybe thet's plenty. An' at least now she can read and write some."

Clark nodded his head. At fifteen Nandry seemed quite capable of caring for a home. Some area young man was bound to welcome her as a helpmate.

So school started again. It was easier this time. Easier to watch Missie go. Easier to put up with the two boys at home, because Nandry was there.

Marty welcomed Nandry's help more than she could express, for in two short months her family would increase again. Nandry, with few words, assumed a great deal of the youngsters' care, taking them with her to feed the chickens, putting Arnie down for his naps—Clare having declared himself too big for such nonsense—and in general assisting with the household duties. Marty greatly appreciated her helpful hands and often told her so.

Then one day as Marty sat in the coolness of the cabin, darning socks, she was surprised by an approaching horse.

Much to her delight, it was Tommie.

"Tommie," she said, "do come in. We haven't seen ya over our way fer jest ages."

Nandry looked up from where she was rolling pie crust dough, flushed, then looked quickly down again. Clare chose this moment of her unguardedness to help himself to a piece of dough.

"How're yer folks?"

"Fine, we all are fine. Thet little Lizzie be growin' like a weed."

"Isn't she a sweetie," Marty said, remembering the last time she had seen little Elizabeth Anne, who was at that time practicing her new learned skill of walking. The tottering steps were awarded with praise, hugs and kisses by doting grandparents and young aunts and uncles.

Marty also recalled that at the same time Rett Marshall was still unable to sit properly alone. A heaviness passed through her and she turned her attention back to Tommie.

"I hear thet ya got yer own land."

"Yep," he said proudly. "Even got a small cabin on it. Not very big, but it should make do fer a while."

"Farmed it yet?"

"Nope. I take over come spring."

A small suspicion raised itself with Marty. Could young Tom be showing interest in her Nandry? Her thoughts were interrupted by Tom's voice.

"Mind taking a little turn outside? It be a first-rate day an' kind of a shame to waste it."

Marty reached for her light shawl.

"Be glad to," she said, "been wantin' to take a little look at the spring afore freeze-up."

She led the way out. At first the conversation was only small talk. They reached the spring and Tom sat down on the cool grass, his back against a tree trunk. Marty watched him. It was clear that something was bothering the boy. Still Tom said nothing. She watched him pick up a piece of bark and break it with his fingers.

"It be a girl, huh?"

He looked up quickly.

"How'd ya know?" he asked.

"It shows," Marty smiled.

"Yeah, guess maybe it does."

He waited a moment then hurried on.

"She's wonderful, Marty—really wonderful. I—I had to talk to someone. Ma wouldn't understand—I know she wouldn't."

Marty was taken aback. What kind of girl wouldn't Ma understand about?

"Maybe yer selling yer ma short?"

"No, I don't think so. Iffen she'd give herself a chance to git to know her—then she'd understand. But, I'm afraid at first—thet's why I came to you, Marty. Ya know Ma. Could ya—could ya talk to her like an'—?"

"Is the girl from around here?"

"Not really. She's—she's from back in the hills. She lives there with her grandfather."

"An' her name?"

"It's Owahteeka."

"O-wah-tee-ka—why, thet sounds like an—" Marty had started her sentence with laughter, but she broke off in shock as the truth grabbed hold of her. Her face went white and she finished lamely.

"She's—Indian."

Tom just nodded.

"Oh, Tommie," Marty said. She wanted to add, "How could you?" but the words wouldn't come, and looking at the anguished face of the young boy, she could say nothing.

She walked away a few steps trying to get things to fall in perspective, but somehow nothing seemed to fit in its proper place.

"Oh, God," she prayed, "please help us work this out."

When she felt that she had herself under control, she returned to Tom, only now she felt the necessity of sitting down. She chose a stump near him and lowered herself to it.

"Okay," she said, "tell me about her."

Tom took a deep breath.

"I met her last fall," he said. "The first time I saw her I was out looking fer a couple of stray cows. They had crawled the fence and gone off into the hill country, an' I went after 'em on horseback. I din't find 'em thet day, but on my way home I found this here saskatoon patch, great big, juicy ones, an' I stopped an' et. An' then I decided to take some to Ma fer a pie, so I took off my hat an' started fillin' it with berries.

"While I was pickin' I could feel eyes lookin' at me, an' I looked up, half expectin' to see a black bear or a cougar, an' there stood this girl—her eyes and her hair were black as a crow's back. She was dressed in buckskin with beads, but what really hit me, she was laughin' at me. Oh, she was tryin' not to, but she was all the same. Her eyes jest—jest lit up like, an' she hid her mouth behind her hand.

"When I asked her what was so funny, she said thet she'd

never seen a brave picking berries like a squaw afore. Thet made me kinda mad, an' I told her thet maybe her braves weren't smart enough to know how good a saskatoon pie tasted.

"She stopped laughin' an' I cooled off some. We talked a bit. She told me her name, 'Owahteeka,' meaning Little Flower. Either way, it sounded pretty.

"We met agin—many times. In the winter months I used to leave her venison or other game. She lives alone with her elderly grandfather. He couldn't stand the reserve so moved back alone to the hills. Owahteeka jest shakes her head when I ask if I can go to her home to meet 'im. He's old—very old. Actually, he is her great-grandfather, an' when he is gone, she won't have no family. She says thet she will go back to the reserve—thet someone will take her in, or thet some brave will make her his wife. But I don't want thet."

He looked directly at Marty now.

"Marty, I want to marry her. I love her. I—" he groaned. "How am I gonna tell Pa and Ma?"

Marty shook her head. Poor Tommie. He who deserved the best girl in the whole west, in love with an Indian.

Marty stood up and pulled her shawl tightly about her, for suddenly the sun didn't seem to be shining as brightly as it had been.

"Oh, Tommie!" she said, shaking her head. "I don't know—I jest don't know."

Tommie, too, got to his feet.

"But ya'll talk to 'em? You'll try—won't ya, Marty?"

"I'll try," she promised. "But Tommie, ya know—ya know it's not gonna be easy—not fer yer folks—not fer enyone."

"I know," he swallowed hard. "I know, but I've thought it all out. I've got my own land, my own cabin. It isn't much, but she's lived the winter in a tent of skins. A cabin should seem good after thet. We won't have to mix much with folks. Our land is sort of off by itself like. We won't bother no one. She'll be close to the hill country—she loves the hills."

"Yer not thinkin' ahead, Tommie," Marty interrupted him. "Yer not thinkin' straight. Babies—family—what about them? Ya can't jest hide 'em in the bush."

Tommie's face darkened.

"Thet's the only answer I don't have," he said. "The only one; but—we'll—we'll work thet out when the time comes."

Marty shook her head.

"Please, Marty," Tom begged; "Please try to talk to Ma. Iffen Ma can see it, she'll convince Pa. Please—"

Marty sighed. "I'll try," she promised, but tears filled her eyes. "I'll honestly try, but I'm not sure how good I'll be at it."

Tommie stepped forward and gave her an impulsive hug.

"Thanks, Marty," he whispered. "Thet's all I ask. An'—an'—someday I'll take ya with me to meet Owahteeka. When you see her, you'll know why—why I feel like I do. Now I gotta run."

He turned to go.

"God, bless Tommie," Marty whispered. She wanted to cover her face and cry.

# Chapter 20

## *Search for a Preacher*

The fall work had been completed, and the farmers' attention could now be turned to other things. A meeting of the community adults was called for on a Saturday afternoon in early October. All residents were invited to attend and very few refused the invitation.

Zeke LaHaye had sent word that though he felt that the meeting was a worthwhile one, he was hard put to keep up with his farm work and just couldn't spare the time.

The neighbors had already discovered that Zeke LaHaye could spare no time from his farming duties—not to honor the Lord's Day, not to help a neighbor, not for any reasons. Clark, who rarely made comment on a neighbor's conduct, confided to Marty: "Thet poor farm sure must be confused-like—first owner contents hisself to let everythin' stay at rest; next owner nigh drives everythin' to death. Makes me stop short-like an' look within. I hope thet I never git so land hungry and money crazy thet I have no time fer God, family, or friends."

Marty silently agreed.

They gathered at the schoolhouse on the predetermined Saturday. Ben Graham was to chair the meeting. When the noise of visiting subsided somewhat, he rose to his feet.

"Friends and neighbors," he began, "I'm sure thet ya all know why this meeting has been called. Fer some time now our area has been without a parson. Twice a year we have the good fortune of having a visiting preacher pass through our neighborhood an' stop long enough to preach us a sermon and marry our young men and women.

"We of the area are concerned thet this ain't enough to give our young'uns the proper-like trainin' in the ways of the Lord.

"A few of us met a while back and talked it over, an' we feel thet it be time to take some action.

"We has us a schoolhouse now. This here fine buildin' is a tribute to what we can do when we work together.

"Now's the time fer us to go to work together agin."

Some people began to applaud and others cheered. It flustered Ben somewhat, but he soon recovered, cleared his throat and went on.

"What we need to do at this point is to choose us two or three men to form a committee to look into the gittin' of a preacher. One thet will stay right here fer regular-like services, fer the buryin' an' the marryin' enytime of the year."

Again people applauded. Ben looked to Ma for support. He must have felt it, for he raised his hand for silence, and then went on.

"We're gonna take names now as to who ya would like. The committee can be two men—or three, iffen ya like. Enymore then thet makes it a bit cumbersome."

A man near the back stood and named Clark Davis. Marty heard several "ayes" for the nominee.

Todd Stern named Ben Graham, and again people voiced approval and heads nodded.

Mr. Coffins then stood and in a loud voice named Mr. Wilbur Whittle. Silence followed. No one in the room knew of what religious bent Mr. Whittle might be. Feet shuffled, throats cleared.

Ben stepped forward.

"Ya all have heard Mr. Coffin's choice. Mr. Whittle, are ya willin' to let yer name stand to help in the selectin' of a new preacher?"

Mr. Whittle rose grandly.

"I believe that I have many connections in the East that could indeed be of great assistance to the men on the committee," he said in his carefully modulated voice.

"An' yer willin' to serve?" asked Ben.

"Certainly, certainly," agreed Mr. Whittle. "I believe that a resident minister will be a great asset in our community."

"Thank ya, Mr. Whittle."

"Ya all have heard the three names given: Clark Davis, myself, and Mr. Whittle. What is yer pleasure?"

"So let it be," came a loud voice.

"We will vote," declared Ben; "those in favor aye, those agin, nay." There were no nays.

After the meeting Mr. Whittle sought out Clark and Ben.

"Now, gentlemen," he said, "I am personally acquainted with many seminarians whom I have no doubt could fill our need quite adequately. Do you wish me to act as correspondent on behalf of the committee?"

Ben frowned, but Clark answered.

"I reckon you could do the letter writin' iffen ya wish. First, though, we'd like to know a bit 'bout these here fellas thet you'll be writin' to."

"Certainly, certainly," said Mr. Whittle. "I shall draw up a resumé of each candidate for presentation, and you can do the choosing as to whom you'd like contacted."

"This ah re-su-may," said Clark; "is thet like an acquaintantship?"

"Acquaintantship?" quired Mr. Whittle. Then, "Precisely—precisely."

"You go ahead an' do thet, Mr. Whittle, an' then Ben and me will go over thet there list with ya."

"Fine, gentlemen, fine," said Mr. Whittle and strutted away quite pleased with himself. He had heard so much back East about the westerner not letting the easterner into the inner circle. Yet here he was, just out a year, and on an important committee—a very important committee—and after his contribution here, his place would be secure, he was sure. He would go to his roominghouse, to his room, close the door and wrack his brain for the best possible candidates he could come up with. Scholars—he knew lots of scholars and some who would even be willing, just as he himself had been, to venture west to taste of the excitement of opening a new frontier. It had its drawbacks, he was willing to admit, but there were compensations. One of them, in his case, being Tessie LaHaye. Back East the ladies had the nasty habit of turning their backs when they saw him approaching. Tessie entertained no such coyness. True, she was barely eighteen, and he thirty-two, but in the West people seemed to quibble less about such details. He was willing to accept her as a very pleasant young lady, and she seemed equally willing to accept him as an eligible man. In fact he felt that she was rather impressed with his bowler hat and white spats. He planned to make a call on Tessie—he hoped very soon, for he was anxious to discover just where he stood. And this meeting had given him the added confidence he needed.

# Chapter 21

## *Marty Talks to Ma*

Marty had put off the much dreaded visit to see Ma, but she knew that she must force herself to make the call. Tommie was counting on her and she had given her promise. Soon winter with its cold and snow would have them locked in its grip, and then she would find the trip difficult physically as well as emotionally.

"What can I use as an excuse?" she asked herself, and could come up with nothing. Finally she just decided to go.

Clark was heading for town for his usual Saturday trip and Marty decided that now was the time.

"Thought thet I'd trail along iffen it not be upsettin' enythin'," she informed him.

He looked pleased. "My pleasure," he said. "Isn't often enough thet I git to show off my wife in town."

"Oh, I'll not be goin' on into town," she quickly corrected. "I'm a plannin' on stoppin' off to chat with Ma while ya be gone."

His pleasure faded somewhat, but not altogether. "Well, at least I'll have me yer company fer a spell," he said.

Marty informed the girls of her plans. Nandry seemed almost happy to have the place to herself.

Marty put on her heavy coat and tied on her bonnet. Her coat wouldn't button properly, so she had to be content to just pull it about her.

Clark eyed her as she crawled heavily up into the wagon, clumsy in spite of his helping hands.

"Ya sure this be the proper time to be a takin' a bumpy wagon ride?" he asked.

"Won't hurt me none," Marty assured him.

Still she noticed that he drove more slowly than usual.

Ma's surprise at seeing Marty was quickly replaced by pleasure.

"I'm so glad thet ya came whilst ya still could," she said, and Marty was sure that Ma thought that her reason for coming was simply that this would be her last opportunity for a while.

They visited, both ladies working on knitting as they chatted. Marty kept one eye on the clock. She mustn't put her purpose for coming off too long and be cut short by Clark's return, or the interruption of some of Ma's family. Finally she took a deep breath and began.

"Tommie came to see me a while back."

Ma looked up, more at the sound of Marty's voice than the words themselves.

"He needed to talk," Marty went on.

Silence.

"A girl, huh?"

"Yeah. Ya knew thet?"

"I thought as much—it shows, ya know. He's got all the signs, but I can't figure it. He ain't said nothin' at all 'bout her. I've tried to lead in thet direction a few times, but he shys away."

Silence again.

"Somethin' be wrong about it; is thet it, Marty?"

Marty swallowed hard.

"No, not wrong, really. Jest—well, jest different—different."

"Different how?"

Marty nearly choked. "Well, this here girl thet Tommie loves—an' he truly does love her, Ma—I saw thet by the way he talked—the way he looked—well, this here girl—her name is—is Owahteeka."

Marty looked quickly at Ma to see if she'd catch the significance. She did. Her needles ceased clicking, her face blanched white, and her eyes filled with horror.

"Tommie?" she said incredulously.

"Yeah, well—ya see, Ma." Marty now felt the need to hurry an explanation, "Tommie didn't mean to meet an Indian girl. Ya see, he was jest lookin' fer stray cows, out in the hill country, an' he stopped at a berry patch to pick ya some berries fer pie. An'—an' this girl was there too, pickin' berries, an' they started talkin', an' then they got better acquainted—over the months like. An'—well—Tommie loves her."

Ma laid aside her knitting and rose to her feet.

"But he can't, Marty, he mustn't. Don't ya see thet? It jest doesn't work. It always means hurt—always."

"I see," Marty said slowly, "but Tommie doesn't."

"What did he say? Don't the girl's people care?"

"She doesn't have people—thet is, no one but an old man—a great-grandfather. They haven't told 'im. Owahteeka thinks it wise to wait," Marty finished lamely.

"Wise to wait, huh," repeated Ma. "Then thet'll stop 'im from doin' somethin' foolish. There be somethin' more then we know?"

"I don't know,"said Marty. "The way thet Tommie talked, I don't think the old man will be around long. An'—an'—I don't think thet she plans to tell him—jest wait 'til he's gone—an' then go ahead. Thet's what I think."

"Oh, dear God," Ma prayed, "what ever are we gonna do?"

Marty slumped in her chair. Who was she to try to give advice to a woman like Ma Graham?

"Well, seems to me," she said, weighing every word, "ya have only a couple a choices. Ya can fight it an' lose Tommie, or ya can okay it and welcome an Indian daughter-in-law."

"Oh, dear God!" said Ma, her face going even whiter.

Ma paced the floor between the table and the stove. Marty waited. Suddenly Ma's face began to restore its color.

"Marty," she said, "I jest thought me of a third choice. I won't fight it an' I won't encourage it, but I sure am goin' to do some prayin'."

"Prayin', how?"

"Prayin'—how do ya think?" The words fairly snapped from Ma. "It jest won't work, Marty. Never. An' I won't have my Tom hurt—shunned an' ridiculed. Grandchildren thet ain't grandchildren 'cause they're neither white nor brown. It ain't to happen, Marty."

"Iffen ya pray like thet, Ma," Marty spoke quietly, slowly, "will ya be askin' fer help or jest givin' orders?"

Ma stiffened. Tears slid down her cheeks. She did not bother to wipe them away. Finally the battle within her seemed to subside. She sat down heavily in the chair across from Marty.

"Yer right—course. I'd like to pray thet God would jest quickly put an end to all this. It scares me, Marty. Truly, it does. I jest feel thet no good can come out of it—no matter what. I'll pray—I'll pray lots, an' I'll try hard to say 'Thy will be done' an' mean it. But I'll tell ya now, Marty—my God's not willin' folks of different races to be marryin' an' raisin' young'uns thet don't belong nowhere. God ain't fer bringin' confusion of either ideas or skins—nor hurt an' pain of bein' shut out—put down. Thet ain't of God, Marty."

Ma stopped her discourse and sat rubbing her work-worn hands together in agitation.

"Me an' Ben gotta have a long talk on this. Then the two of us will try an' talk some sense into Tommie. He's too good a boy, Marty—too good to lose like this."

Marty only nodded. She felt as though she had not done what she had come to do. She wished that Ma had left just a wee small crack in the door instead of closing it so firmly, but maybe Ma was right. Who was she, Marty, to know the proper way to handle such a situation? And surely as Ma spent time in prayer, if she were wrong, it would be revealed to her. But it might take time.

Poor Tommie. Marty's heart ached for him. Somehow she felt that no matter how things went, there was heartache in store for the boy. If only there were some way to spare him the hurt. She hoped that Clark would hurry back from town. She was anxious to pour it all out to him on the quiet ride home.

# Chapter 22

# *A Call on Wanda*

Marty was busy at the kitchen cupboard making Clark's favorite dessert. Clare came in from outside, pulled up a chair and watched her.

"Are ya mad at Pa?"

Marty stopped rolling the dough and looked at the boy. "Whatcha meanin'?"

"Thet's his favorite," explained Clare. "Ya always make his favorite when ya been mad."

He jumped down and was gone before Marty could even answer. He had laid the words out very matter-of-factly, as though they bore no consequence and needed no explaining. Marty frowned. It was a while before the rolling pin again went to work on the dough.

"Do I really do thet?" she asked herself. "An' iffen I do, is it thet obvious?"

The fact was, she hadn't had a fuss with Clark at all. She was just paving the way to ask him for the team so that she might pay an afternoon call on Wanda. Now Clark was not one to keep his woman holed up at home, but he did have some strange notions when it neared her confinement time, and Marty had visions of Clark advising her to stay put for the present. Maybe his favorite dessert would put him in a more pliable mood, she had reasoned, and then this smart young

Clare had come along. If he could see through her so easily, might not Clark?

Marty put the dessert in the oven with a new lack of confidence. Maybe she was foolish to even approach Clark, but she wanted so much to have a talk with Wanda.

Talk was gradually making its way from neighbor to neighbor that something was indeed wrong with the Marshall child, and Marty held her breath lest it get back to Cam and Wanda. She knew there was no wall of protection that she could build, but if she could just learn if Wanda was aware that her small son was—different. Marty felt that Wanda's acceptance of the fact would be her own protective wall—the only thing that could shield her from the hurt.

The dessert baked to perfection and Clark picked up the aroma even before he stepped through the kitchen door.

"Umm," he called ahead, "apple turnovers. Makes a man's mouth water."

Marty smiled, but still felt unsure. Nandry led Arnie in and washed him at the hand basin, and they joined Clark and Clare at the table.

The meal was pleasant but hurried. Clark had pressing work to which he wished to return. Marty knew that she must not waste time.

"Ya be a needin' the team this afternoon?"

Clark gave her a sharp look.

"Ya plannin' on pickin' rock?"

Marty felt the warmth rise into her cheeks, but she bit back the cutting remark she wanted to respond with and instead spoke quietly, her voice well controlled.

"I thought as how I'd like to take me a quick trip to see Wanda."

"It may be a mite quicker then you'd planned."

Marty got the implication with no difficulty.

"Oh, Clark," she said in disgust, "I been through this before. Now don't ya think if my time was close thet I'd be a knowin' it?"

Clark looked unconvinced. "As *sudden* travail cometh upon a woman," he quoted, emphasizing the word sudden.

Marty was sure that she had lost.

Clark finished his coffee in silence and rose to go.

"Tell ya what," he said, stopping to put on his coat; "iffen ya be so set on seein' Wanda, I'll drive ya on over."

"But yer work," said Marty.

"It'll keep."

"But it's not at all that necessary. I'd be jest fine on my own. Honest, Clark, there be no need—"

"It's my drivin' or not at all—take yer pick," Clark said with finality.

Marty swallowed a big lump of anger. He was so stubborn. Most as bad as Jedd Larson.

"Okay," she said finally, her anger still showing. "Okay, I'd be much obliged iffen ya'd drive me over."

"I'll be ready in fifteen minutes," Clark said and went for the team.

Marty turned to the table and vented some of her anger on the dirty dishes.

"Ya gonna make another apple 'sert, Ma?" asked Clare.

Marty felt like swatting him.

"An' you, boy," she said, "you go out an' haul in some firewood. Fill up the woodbox—right to the top—an' be quick 'bout it, too."

Clare went. Marty knew that she had been unfair. Clare was used to hauling wood, and goodness knew it wouldn't hurt him any, but she hadn't needed to be so mean about it.

The ride to the Marshalls was a fairly silent one. Marty still felt peevish and Clark did not try to draw her out. When they arrived, Clark went on to the barn where he saw Cam working on harnesses, and Marty went in to see Wanda. Young Rett lay on the floor on a blanket. Wanda's eyes shone as she spoke of him.

"He can sit up real good now," she told Marty and went about demonstrating.

"But Wanda," Marty wanted to protest, "the boy be a year and a half old. He should be walkin'—no, runnin'. He should be runnin' after his pa and sayin' words. And here you be, gloryin' in the fact that he can finally sit."

But Marty did not say it. She merely smiled her approval

at Rett's great achievement. Wanda talked on enthusiastical-
ly, and soon the men joined them.

They were seated at the crowded little table when Marty
felt the first pain. It caught her by surprise and she stiffened
somewhat. She was soon able to relax again and hoped that no
one had noticed. When the next one came a few minutes later,
she felt eyes upon her and looked up to see Clark watching her.
She knew without comment that he was aware.

Clark refused a second cup of coffee and said that they
really must be hurrying home.

Cam, still bragging about his boy, pushed back from the
table and went with Clark for his team.

Marty smiled bravely as she bid Wanda farewell, and
prayed that Clark would please hurry.

In short order the team was at the door, and Clark jumped
down to help Marty into the wagon.

They travelled home at a much brisker pace than they had
travelled to the Marshalls'.

"Are ya gonna make it?" Clark asked at one point and
Marty nodded.

"I sent Cam for the Doc."

Marty felt thankfulness flow through her.

Baby Elvira arrived safely, in Doc's presence and in her
mother's bed, at precisely 5:20 that afternoon.

Missie, Clare and Arnie were all impressed with the tiny
bundle. Even Clae and Nandry showed excitement at welcoming the new little girl.

"Can we call her Elvira, Ma?" Missie asked.

"Iffen ya like," said Marty.

"Good. I read a story about an Elvira in a book of Mr.
Whittle's. I think thet it's a nice name."

This was the first time that Marty had not had Ma present
at the arrival of an offspring and in the days immediately following. Nandry took over the running of the house, and a first-
rate job she did. Marty couldn't believe the young girl's effi-
ciency.

"Nandry," she said with sincerity, "I jest don't know how
we ever managed without ya."

Nandry allowed herself a brief, small smile.

# Chapter 23

# *The New Preacher*

Mr. Whittle was taking his job as committee member very seriously. He had drawn up careful descriptions of each likely candidate, including their background, disposition and education and presented it to Clark and Ben.

From the eight names presented, the committee chose three they felt might be possibilities. Mr. Whittle, as contact man, was then commissioned to write the necessary letters. He did so with great flourish, describing in detail the community, the great pioneer fervor of its settlers, and their depth of religious convictions. The letters were sent off in due course and the answers awaited with a great deal of expectancy and some trepidation.

The letter finally arrived from candidate A. He was much enamored by the prospects, but after much prayer, he did not feel the Lord leading in that direction. Ben took this to mean that the promised salary was not enough.

Then they heard from candidate C. He, too, found it difficult to resist such a splendid opportunity, but he was getting married in a month's time, and as his wife-to-be was a very delicate little thing, he felt that he could not possibly ask her to move so far away from the comforts of the city. "Kinda likes his soft chair and slippers," mused Ben. Candidate B was finally heard from. He had considered the proposal with great care, had taken much time to think about it, and perhaps in the future he would be able to consider it, but for the present he was still unable to give a final answer. "So he's hopin' fer somethin' bigger," said Ben and struck candidate B from his list as well.

Again the remaining five were considered. To Clark and Ben they didn't look like the kind of men that would fit their need, but the schoolteacher was so sure of their capabilities.

"Take the Reverend Watson here," he said with enthusiasm. "He has just graduated from seven years of study for the ministry. He would be a splendid minister."

Clark and Ben couldn't help but wonder what had taken him so long, but finally consented to allow Mr. Whittle to contact the man as well as a Rev. Thomas whose name appeared on the list.

After some length of time the Rev. Watson declared that he was most eager to take the gospel to the people of sin-darkened western territory.

With the prospect of a minister who was willing to come, a meeting of the community was called to make final plans and preparations.

It was decided that he, too, would board at the Watleys'. Mr. Whittle's room was a large one and could accommodate another single bed and an extra desk. Mr. Whittle was delighted with this. It would be so good to renew acquaintance with the good Reverend, and it would be such a boost to his morale to have a stimulating conversation mate. Really, there was a great lack of intellectuals in this community. Then, too, his calling on the young Tessie had been accepted with favor, and he was most anxious to have someone to whom he could boast, just a little bit.

All in all, it was a most pleasant arrangement, and Mr. Whittle looked forward, in a personal way, to the coming of the new minister.

The Sunday meetings would be held in the schoolhouse. It would be cramped but they could squeeze in, so long as there was no need to move about.

Everyone bubbled with excitement at the prospect of their

very own minister. It would be so good to have someone there permanently. In times of birth, death, or marriage, that's when a minister was needed—not just once or twice a year as he passed through the area.

Secretly, the good teacher hoped that it would not be too long before he personally would be putting to work the marrying talents of the new man.

True, he had a few things to work out yet—like where to live with a new bride. He could hardly move her in with him at the Watleys', though the thought had occurred to him. However, he was confident that these things would work themselves out.

The arrangements were made to bring the new parson out, and the people eagerly looked forward to the first meeting. The date was set for March 15, and the winter months promised to pass quickly.

# Chapter 24

## *Tommie*

Shortly after Ellie arrived, Marty had a call from Ma. It was so good, not just to show off the new baby girl, but also to have a chance for a nice long chat. Ma's visit was full of news. Her face was flushed with it.

"I declare, Marty," she beamed as they settled to a cup of coffee, "I'm gonna have me another son-in-law."

Marty looked up in surprise.

"Really?" She caught some of the excitement from Ma. "Nellie?"

"Yeah, Nellie."

"I didn't know."

"Not many did. Don't know much about it myself. Nellie doesn't say much, an' the young man—well, I'm still marvellin' thet he finally got it said, him being as tight-lipped as he is."

"Who—?"

"Shem Vickers."

"No!"

Ma nodded with a grin.

" 'Magine thet. Never even really got to know the boy 'til the last few weeks. He's right nice—even if he don't have much to say."

Marty giggled. "Don't s'pose the poor fellow ever had a

chance to develop his talking skills much. He sure oughta have first-rate ears though—iffen they're not already weared out."

Ma grinned silently.

"Yeah, Mrs. Vickers can talk 'nough fer a crowd."

"When's the weddin' to be?"

"Most as soon as thet new parson gits here. Prob'ly April."

Marty smiled.

"Well, thet's really nice. I'm so happy fer 'em both."

Ma agreed.

"Nellie been a right fine girl. I'm gonna miss her, but she's all excited-like with the plans fer a place of her own."

"She'll make Shem a fine little wife, I'm sure o' thet."

Marty passed Ma the cookies and then asked. "Ma, have Ben and you talked over 'bout Tommie yet?"

Ma nodded, the happiness fading some from her face. "Yeah, we talked 'bout it. Then we talked to Tom, too. Ben, he doesn't seem too upset 'bout it. Oh, he was at first, but then he sorta jest seemed to think—what'll be, will be. But it ain't right, Marty. It will only mean hurt. I don't want Tommie hurt—nor the girl either, fer thet matter. Oh, I wisht it were all a bad dream."

Ma stopped and sat shaking her head, her eyes downcast.

"I'm sure thet it will work out," said Marty, trying to sound confident. "Tommie's a smart boy. Iffen it's not gonna work, he'll know it."

"Tommie is too 'gone' to see enything," Ma replied. "Never saw a young man so dew-struck. Tommie wants to bring her to the house to meet Ben and me."

"Why shouldn't he?"

"I don't know, Marty. Seems iffen we say he can, we sorta open the door fer the other, too. An' the kids—how ya think they'd all feel—seein' Tommie with an Indian. An' sure thing they wouldn't be able to keep it quiet-like either—babble it round the school an' all. The whole area round would know 'bout it. It's jest not good—not good at all."

Marty ached for Ma, but she also hurt for Tommie. There just didn't seem to be any way out without someone hurting.

"Ma, I think I'd like to have a chat with Tom agin. Could ya send him on over when he's got a minute?"

"Sure—guess chattin' won't hurt nothin'."

"Tell ya what," said Marty. "I'll send along a note with ya. Fer Tom. Thet be okay?"

Ma looked surprised, but agreed.

"It'll jest take a minute," said Marty and poured Ma another cup of coffee as she spoke.

"Ya jest enjoy yer coffee an' I'll be right back."

She went to the bedroom and found a sheet of paper and a pencil.

"Dear Tom," she wrote. "I think it would be good iffen ya could bring Owahteeka to see me. Come next Wednesday, if ya can. Yer friend, Marty."

Carefully she folded the sheet and returned to the kitchen. Ma tucked the note into a pocket and made no comment. Marty knew that the short letter would be handed over to Tom.

# Chapter 25

## *School News*

The afternoon sun seemed weak and anemic as it shone listlessly on the winter snow. A cold wind had arisen and Marty fretted over the children having to tramp home from school in the cold.

She watched nervously at the window for the two figures to appear, fearing with a mother's heart that the cold might somehow detain them, or, at best, return them with frostbite.

When they finally came into view, they looked cheerful, chattering as they came, not even seeming in a hurry to get in out of the weather.

Marty met them at the door.

"Aren't ya near froze?" she asked.

Missie looked at her with surprise, then answered casually, "Sure is cold out."

"I know. I was worried."

" 'Bout what?"

" 'Bout you—an' Clae—comin' home in the wind."

"We're all right."

She shrugged out of her coat and had to be reminded to hang it on its peg.

"Here," Marty said, "I've heated some milk. Best warm yerself up a bit."

The girls accepted the warm milk and the slice of cake that went with it.

"It was cold in school today too," offered Clae.

"Yeah," teased Missie, "Nathan gave Clae his sweater to keep warm."

Clae flushed. "Oh, yeah, well, Willie loves you."

"Does not," Missie responded heatedly. "I hate thet Willie LaHaye."

"Well, he don't hate you."

"Does too. We hate each other—him and me."

Clae appeared to be changing the subject, but to Marty's dismay it turned out to be the same old one.

"Know what? Today we had honor time fer the two—boy an' girl—who got the best marks in sums and in spellin'. An' guess who got honored—had to go up front an' stand." Missie was shooting daggers at Clae with her eyes, but Clae ignored them and went on, "—stand right up there while everybody clapped. Guess who? Missie and Willie."

She clapped her hands together with glee and repeated again.

"Missie and Willie."

"I'm proud, Missie, thet ya got top marks," Marty cut in, hoping to divert the conversation, but it didn't work.

"Missie and Willie," Clae said again. "Bet ya get married when ya grow up."

"We will not." Missie bounded off her chair, spilling the remainder of her milk. "I'm gonna marry Tommie, Clae Larson, an' don't ya fergit it." She was in tears now and as a final vent to her anger she reached for a handful of Clae's hair and yanked hard before she ran off to her room.

Now Clae's tears flowed.

Marty's intervention was too late to stop the initial outburst. She tried to comfort Clae, at the same time admonishing her not to tease Missie so much, wiped up the spilled milk and went to talk to her daughter.

Missie was hard to convince that the hair-pulling was not in order—a just dessert for the actions of Clae. Marty firmly informed her that it was not to happen again. The hardest part of the talking came when Marty explained, as kindly as she knew how, that Tommie was a man full grown, and he might have other ideas as to whom he wished to marry. This was hard for Missie to comprehend. Tommie had always been her "good pal."

"I know," said Marty, "but 'good pals' don't always grow up and git married. 'Specially when one is a grown man already and the other a little girl."

"Then I'll never, ever marry anyone," Missie vowed, "not iffen I can't marry Tommie."

Marty smoothed her hair and said she s'posed thet would be fine—but if Missie ever changed her mind, that was okay too.

Missie finally wiped away the last of her tears and at her mother's bidding went to offer her apology to Clae.

# Chapter 26

## *Owahteeka*

Wednesday arrived. Tom appeared at Marty's door. At her bid to come in, Tom interposed.

"Would ya all mind comin' out," he asked, "back to the spring? We'd rather see ya private-like."

Marty bundled up and followed him.

Clark was away, Ellie sound asleep, and Nandry had Clare and Arnie occupied.

The air was crisp, but the wind was down, so the cold was not as penetrating.

Marty and Tom moved along the path to the spring without speaking. Marty wondered just what to expect. What would the girl at the other end of the trail be like? What was there about her to make Tommie fall so in love?

As she approached the appointed spot, a slim figure clad in beaded buckskins turned to meet her.

"She's beautiful," was Marty's first thought, and looked from the deep black eyes to the sensitive face. Her lips were slightly parted, and she stood there silently, measuring Marty, even as Marty tried in a moment's time to measure her.

"Owahteeka," said Marty softly, letting a smile warm her face, and reaching out a hand, "I'm right glad to meet ya."

Owahteeka softened too.

"And I," she spoke carefully, "I am happy to meet you—Marty. Tom has told me much about you."

Marty's eyes widened in surprise.

"Ya speak English—very well."

"I went to a mission school when my mother still lived," she explained, showing little feeling about the matter.

"An' yer mother—?"

"Is gone. I now live only with my grandfather. He did not wish me in the mission school."

"I see."

Tom had moved beside Owahteeka. His eyes shone with love. He had been sure that Marty would understand and love her, and his heart beat more quickly, willing it to be so.

"Has Tommie met yer grandfather?"

"Oh, no," she said quickly; "he must not."

"I'd like to," said Tom. "I'd like to talk to the old man, tell 'im—"

"He does not speak nor understand the white man's tongue," broke in Owahteeka.

"Well, then," said Tom, "at least I could shake his hand—could smile."

"No." Owahteeka shook her head firmly. "You must not. My grandfather—he would not wish to meet you."

"But Marty has met you. She's white an'—"

Owahteeka's dark eyes flashed. "The white lady did not lose her sons and grandsons to Indian arrows, as my grandfather lost his to the white man's bullets."

Marty stepped forward and placed her hand on the young girl's arm.

"We understand," she said. "Tom will not try to see yer grandfather—not now enyway. But can—can you *always* hide your love?" She waved a hand to include the two young people. "Can ya hide it from '*im*?"

"My grandfather is very old," said Owahteeka softly. "He is very old and weak. He will soon go to his fathers—there is no need to tell him."

"I see." So her guess had been right.

As silence followed, Marty fumbled for the right words,

and finally just blurted it out.

"An' you, Owahteeka, do you wish to—to marry Tommie?"

"Oh, yes." The dark eyes softened as Owahteeka looked at the young man beside her. Tommie's arms encircled her. Who could deny the love that passed between them?

Marty swallowed a lump in her throat and turned to walk away a few paces. She came back slowly again. Her heart ached for the young people before her—of different culture, of different religions, of different skin. Why did they make it so difficult for themselves? What could she say or do?

She found her voice.

"Owahteeka, I think I understand why Tommie loves ya. You're a beautiful, sensitive girl. I—I wish thet I could feel thet—thet life will treat ya kindly iffen ya marry. I don't know. I really don't know."

She looked up then into the perceptive eyes of the girl before her. "But this I want ya to always know. Ya can count on me fer a friend."

"Thank you," whispered Owahteeka. Marty stepped forward and embraced the girl, looked deep into Tommie's eyes and turned back down the path to the house.

Tears fell as she walked. Her heart felt heavy. She'd talk with Ma. She still didn't know if it was right for her to interfere. She wouldn't try to persuade Ma that the marriage was the right thing, but she would try to make Ma see that Tommie's choice was understandable.

# Chapter 27

# *Bits 'n Pieces*

When Clark went to town the following Saturday, he returned with the sobering news that Mrs. McDonald was gravely ill. The Doc, who had been faithfully attending her, reported her problem as a severe stroke. One side was paralyzed, her speech was gone, and she was confined to her bed in serious condition. No hope for her complete recovery was given.

Mrs. Nettles and Widow Gray, from town, took turns with Mr. McDonald in round-the-clock nursing. The store had been put up for sale.

Marty felt sick at heart upon hearing the news. She had never liked Mrs. McDonald, and the news of her illness filled her with guilt feelings.

"Maybe iffen I'd really tried," she told herself, "maybe I could have found a lovable woman behind the pryin' eyes and probin' tongue."

But there was little relief to her in the "maybes."

"God," she prayed, "please forgive me. I've been wrong. Help me in the future to see good in all people. To mine it out like, iffen it seems buried deep."

She sent a roast and a pie along with her condolences to Mr. McDonald. That was about the extent of the amends that she could make.

The winter months passed by, and the time for the coming

of the new preacher was drawing near.

Nellie's wedding plans were progressing favorably. Shem Vickers seemed to find his tongue and was talking more than he had probably done in all his previous years on earth. He seemed to take great pleasure in spreading the word that he was soon to be a groom.

Mr. Wilbur Whittle was also making progress with his courtship, but he had given up the prospects of being the first one to the altar. He still hadn't solved his problem of where to live, so had withheld asking the fateful question. Tessie, not understanding what was holding him back, was becoming rather impatient.

Mr. Whittle finally dared to approach the committee who served as the school board, to request that a residence be acquired at the school site. He supplied them with a list of the reasons why such a move would be advantageous.

He would be there to watch the fire in the winter.

He would be available should a student require his services, apart from school hours.

It would mean less time spent on the road, et cetera.

None of the reasons that he gave was the real one, but the board after some consideration decided that a resident teacher may not be a bad idea and voted to take out logs over the next winter to construct a modest but adequate building come the next spring.

It was a step in the right direction, but it seemed so far in the future. Mr. Whittle had hoped for action a bit sooner. He deemed it wise, for the time, to hold his tongue as far as his intention toward Miss Tessie LaHaye.

And so the matter lay. Tessie didn't exactly give up—but she did become agitated.

## Chapter 28

# *Owahteeka and Ma*

Marty bundled Ellie against the spring wind and set off for the Grahams. She felt that she must have her visit with Ma.

Nandry kept Clae and Arnie at home. Marty had suggested that they all take the air together but Nandry politely refused. "She should get out more," Marty worried. "She's getting to be a real loner," but the company of the two small children seemed to be enough for Nandry.

The Graham house seemed quiet. With a family swarming through the rooms, it was usually a bustle of activity, but now with the youngsters off to school and Tom out working round the farm buildings, only Nellie was left to keep Ma company. She laid aside the towels that she was hand-stitching and came to take the wee Ellie.

"Did ya know thet Sally Anne be expectin' another—not till fall. This time Jason is hopin' fer a boy, though he sure wouldn't trade thet Elizabeth Anne fer an army of boys."

Marty smiled. An addition to the family was always good news.

"How's Sally Anne keepin'?"

"Fine. She's busy as can be carin' fer Jason and thet girl of hers."

Nellie laid the baby in a cradle kept for little visitors, one small granddaughter in particular, and went to put on the coffee.

Marty was then shown all of the household items that Nellie had prepared for her new home. Ma was piecing another quilt. Marty wondered who was enjoying the coming event the most, Nellie or Ma.

The coffee was ready and they each took up their sewing and prepared to visit.

They shared news from the neighborhood, expressed their concern for the McDonalds, and discussed in detail Nellie's coming wedding.

When there was a lull, Marty brought up the subject that she had really come to discuss.

"Tommie came last week—like I asked him to."

Ma nodded. "Yeah, he said he'd seen ya."

"Did he also say that he brought a friend?"

"Nope."

"Owahteeka." Marty let the name drop, and waited a moment.

Ma's head jerked up in surprise and Nellie's needle stopped in midair.

"I asked 'im to," Marty went on. "I felt thet somebody should meet her an' git to know jest what kind of a girl she be. I knew thet it was awkward-like fer her to come here, but no matter to my place."

Ma's eyes were asking Marty to hurry on—to tell her what the girl was like. Nellie asked it.

"What's she like?"

"She's beautiful. It ain't a wonder thet young Tom fell so hard. She's tiny and straight as a willow. She's slim and brown, with big black eyes an' long black braids. She's edjecated, too; speaks English real good. She's polite—an'—"

"Oh, God!" whispered Ma, laying aside her sewing and bowing her head. "What are we gonna do?"

Marty stopped at the interruption and the three sat in silence, each nursing her own thoughts; then Marty went on.

"But she's hurtin', too. She loves Tommie—I'm sure o' thet. But I think—I think maybe thet be the only white man thet she loves—or trusts either. Her grandfather—he—he hates the white and with good cause, maybe. He took her from the mission school. I don't really think thet she even liked me. Fer Tommie's sake she tried to, but the doubtin' was still in her eyes."

Marty waited.

"Still, she did try—fer Tommie. An' maybe—in time—I jest don't know."

Ma had not lifted her head. She passed a calloused hand over her face.

"Iffen I only knew what to do. Iffen I only knew," she moaned.

Nellie was quick to cut in.

"Don't seem no problem to me," she pointed out. "Iffen they love each other, why shouldn't they marry?"

Ma looked up. "Indeed, young Nell," she said. "All you be a seein' right now is love. Me—I see beyond—to heartache an' shunnin' an' a family not white nor brown."

Ellie fussed and Marty rose to get her. Had she said the right things? she wondered. Should she fight for the young couple? No, she didn't have the right, nor the wisdom, to know if it was proper. She had told them how she saw the Indian girl—her strength, her love, her doubts. Now Ma would have to take it from there.

## Chapter 29

# *The New Preacher Arrives*

A team and wagon was sent to the nearby center of trade to pick up the new preacher and bring him to the town. He was to spend two days at the small hotel getting rested after his long trip and then he would be transported to the Watleys' where he would make his abode. Belle Watley was all in a dither. Imagine! Not only did she have the distinguished honor of housing the schoolteacher but now the new preacher as well. However, Belle did not believe in letting her excitement influence her activities, and though her chatter and color intensified, she was still content to let her daughters do the bustling about.

Word that the sent-out wagon had indeed "got its man" spread quickly. The Reverend was resting as planned in the nearby hotel and would be picked up by the Watleys for residence at their farmstead on the following Friday. This would give him a day to settle in and prepare himself for the Lord's Day and the first meeting with his new congregation.

The whole neighborhood felt the excitement, and on Sunday morning the teams and wagons began to stream into the schoolyard. Even the unfaithful members of the flock turned out, except for Zeke LaHaye, though he allowed his wife and family a few hours off so that they, too, might take in the service.

Marty was prepared to see another small man like the teacher, thinking that perhaps that was the way they made them out East. She was thus unprepared for the sight of the still young Rev. Watson. He was tall, but that was not his outstanding feature. It was his size! It wasn't exactly the weight that the Reverend carried that surprised her, but how—or rather where—he carried it. Somehow it seemed to be all bunched out front. His suitcoat was hard put trying to keep the front of him covered, and his face looked like a small round replica of what was stored somewhere below his chest. Round and full it was, and no one was quite sure if the Reverend had a neck.

Seeing a round face made one expect that it should appear jolly—but not so the Rev. Watson. Marty had never beheld such a stern face. There were no laugh lines there, no crinkles at the corners of the eyes.

"Maybe he still be weary," she told herself. "By next Sunday he'll likely be more hisself."

The good Reverend possessed a booming voice, and in spite of the fact that some of the hymns were unfamiliar, the singing went well. The prayer too was very meaningful to Marty. It was so good to be able to worship in this way, to have regular spiritual instruction for her growing children.

The sermon left Marty puzzled. The Reverend had a voice that was easy enough to listen to, though he did at times get a mite loud. It was the words that Marty had a problem with. There were so many of them that she didn't understand. Just when she felt that perhaps she knew what he was saying, she would get lost again. She chided herself for her ignorance, and determined to check with Clark on the way home.

There was general chatter and introductions as the people filed out. Marty heard several comments of "Good sermon, Parson," and was more convinced than ever that she was terribly dull.

On the way home she put it to Clark.

"Rev. Watson's jest fine, ain't he?"

"Seems so."

"Got a nice loud voice, hasn't he?"

" 'Deed he has."

"Sings real good, too."

"Fine singer."

"Clark—what *was* he talkin' 'bout?"

Clark fairly howled.

"Be hanged iffen I know," he finally managed.

"Ya don't know either?"

"Haven't a notion," said Clark. "Don't s'pose there be a soul there who did."

"Thought it was jest me thet's dumb," admitted Marty, and Clark laughed again.

"Well," he said, getting himself under control, "I think the good parson was sayin' somethin' about man bein' a special creature, designed fer a special purpose, but I never did get rightly sorted out what thet purpose was. 'Fulfillment of self-image' or some such thing seems to have come up more than once. Not sure what he be a meanin'."

Marty sat quietly.

"Maybe next Sunday he'll explain," she said thoughtfully.

## Chapter 30

# *Leavin'*

Marty was clearing away the supper dishes when she heard a horse approaching. It was Tommie and he seemed in a great hurry. Marty prayed that nothing was wrong as she hurried to meet him.

His face was white and drawn and there was a determined set to his chin.

"Can I see ya?" he asked briskly.

"Of course, Tommie," she said drawing him in, then added quickly, "Tommie, what's wrong?"

"I'm leavin'."

"Leavin! Fer where? Why?"

"I'm goin' west."

"But why?"

"I got a note this afternoon from Owahteeka. We were to meet as usual but she wasn't there. I waited an' waited an' I got worried, an' then jest as I was gonna go find her—grandfather or no—I spotted these stones piled up—an' in 'em a letter."

He shoved the crumpled paper toward Marty and she took it with shaking hands.

"Dear Tommie,

Grandfather must have learned of us. He is taking me back to the reservation. Please don't try to follow. It would mean danger. I am promised to Running Deer for his wife.

Owahteeka."

Marty could understand now the anguish in the young man's face.

"Oh, Tommie!" she whispered. "I'm sorry."

Tom shuffled around, and Marty realized that he was fighting for control.

"But why—why go away?"

"I won't stay here." There was bitterness in his voice. "Thet's jest what Ma wanted. She should be happy now."

Marty laid a hand on the trembling arm.

"Tommie, no mother is ever happy when their young'uns hurt. Can't ya see thet? Oh, I know Ma was worried, worried 'bout you an' Owahteeka. She didn't feel it right. But yer hurtin', Tommie—yer hurtin' will never make her happy. She's gonna hurt too, Tommie—truly she is."

Tommie wiped the back of his hand across his face, and half turned from Marty.

"I still gotta go," he finally said. "I jest can't stay here— thet's all. Every day I'll think thet I see Ma lookin' through me, sortin' me out, wishin' me to find another girl—"

"I see," Marty said gently.

"I left 'em a note; didn't say much. You tell 'em, will ya, Marty? Try to tell 'em why I had to go."

Marty agreed with a shake of her head.

"Be careful, Tommie, ya hear—an' write a note now and then, will ya?"

He nodded but said nothing; his voice just wouldn't work. He turned and was gone and Marty was left standing there, watching him go, the tears streaming down her cheeks.

# Chapter 31

## *Time Moves On*

No one took Tom's departure any harder than the young Missie. Many were left aching and hurting because of it, but along with the hurt on Missie's part was a deep confusion. It was simply beyond her to comprehend why Tommie would choose to do such a thing. Marty tried to explain, but her efforts were all in vain.

Ma was helped somewhat over the trying days by the attention that was needed for Nellie's wedding plans.

March was torn from the general store calendar and discarded. April came again, promising new growth, new life, new vigor. Nellie plunged into the last-minute preparations with flushed cheeks and a smiling face.

"Do folks always smile when they gonna marry?" asked Clare after a Sunday morning service in which he had spent more time watching the people than listening to the Reverend.

Marty smiled. "Mostly," she said; "mostly they do."

Clare let it go at that; the "why" of the whole matter quite escaped him.

The Reverend had by now presented five sermons to his congregation, and Marty had long since given up on him explaining his meaning. Others seemed to have given up also, for a few of the less ardent families had ceased to attend. The schoolroom was still overcrowded, however, and the worship service wasn't as worshipful as many wished it to be.

Marty did wish that the Reverend weren't quite so "edje-cated." Her soul longed so much to be fed, and Sunday by Sunday she went home feeling empty. Oh, the words were pretty words, fancy words, and she was sure, very intellec-tual—but so empty to one who could not understand.

They had entertained the Reverend for Sunday dinner. Marty felt that she had found the secret to his strange shape. Never had she seen a man tuck away as much fried chicken or mashed turnips. She said nothing, but when she saw young Clare watching him wide-eyed in disbelief, she suppressed the desire to giggle and quickly diverted Clare's attention lest he blurt out some remark that would bring embarrassment.

They accepted their new minister—accepted him for who he was, for Whom he represented, for what he had come to do. They accepted him, but deep down inside, there was probably no one who cared much for him, though not one of them would have been disloyal enough to say so.

# Chapter 32

## *Rett*

Spring passed into summer, and summer to autumn. School began again, and along with the girls trudged the young Clare, very self-confident and assured. His only concern was how Clark would manage without him. But Clark said "thet he s'posed he could make do—he had Arnie now."

Clare was full of tales of school. Missie often accused him of being a downright tattletale, but that did not dampen Clare's enthusiasm for a good story.

One day Marty sat listening to the quietness of the house as she knitted a new mitten. Nandry was off picking blueberries in the far pasture, Arnie was helping his dad, the three school children were at their classes, and Ellie was having her nap.

Marty's thoughts turned to Wanda. She saw Wanda and Cam fairly frequently. By now the whole community was aware that little Rett was far from normal—everyone, it seemed, but Wanda and Cam. Marty's heart felt heavy as she thought of the boy. He was a big boy for his age. He was walking now, but he still did not attempt to speak, and it was evident that he would never be as other children.

Cam still boasted about his son. How would he take it, Marty wondered, when he finally realized the truth.

Marty was surprised to look up from her reverie and see

Wanda herself driving into the yard.

Wanda had brought Rett with her and he proudly sat beside her on the wagon seat, holding the end of the reins.

Wanda tied the team and lifted the big boy down. He shuffled about the yard and became excited at the sight of Ole Bob. The boy and the dog soon became acquainted.

Then Wanda took the boy's hand and led him toward the house. He did not protest but he did not show any eagerness either.

Wanda wasted no time with small talk.

"I had to see you, Marty," she said. Marty noticed her quivering chin. Wanda plunged right in.

"I know that the neighbors are all talking about Rett being different. I know that they are. I know, too, that they think—that they think Cam and I aren't aware. We know, Marty, we know. I guess I've known from the time that Rett was a small baby. Oh, I hoped and prayed that I'd be wrong—but I knew. For a while I wondered about Cam. I wondered when he'd learn the truth—how he'd feel when he did. And then—one night—one night—well, he just spilled it all out—he'd known, too."

Wanda stopped and her lips trembled. She fought for control for a moment, then went on.

"Marty, have you—have you ever seen a grown man cry? I mean really cry? It's awful—just awful."

Wanda wiped away tears, took a breath and went on bravely.

"I felt that I just had to share with someone—someone who would understand. It was hard at first—really hard. But, Marty, I want you to know that I wouldn't change it, not really. He has brought us so much joy. You see," she looked at Marty, the tears glistening in her eyes, "I asked God so many times for a baby. And—and He's given me one—a—a boy that will, in some respects, never grow up. Now, can I fault God for answering my prayer? I don't suppose, Marty, that Rett will ever leave me, not even for school. I have—I have my baby—for always."

"Oh, Wanda." Marty put her arms around her friend and

they wept together. When their tears had washed away their renewed sorrow and cleansed away the frustration, they were able to look together to the future with new acceptance and anticipation, and even to talk of other things.

Rett played contentedly with the building blocks, pushing them back and forth on the kitchen floor, for he couldn't seem to succeed in stacking them.

Chapter 33

# Plans for a Church

The next spring the small log teacherage was built, and
Mr. Wilbur Whittle and his new bride moved in to take possession. The community had long since realized the real reason, on Mr. Whittle's part, for the home near the schoolhouse,
for immediately after he was assured that it would indeed be
built, he asked for the hand of Miss Tessie. The community
smiled its approval, and as the finishing touches were put on
the cabin, the Reverend Watson did the honors of pronounc-
ing the couple husband and wife.

There was a growing dissatisfaction, however, with the
Sunday morning worship service. Rather than thinking it the
fault of the "learned man," the people looked instead to the
place of meeting. The school was crowded, the seating was inadequate, there was no place to take fussing children. The
whole situation was not conducive to worship.

The general feeling grew and in between the planting of
crops and the haying season, a meeting was called to discuss
the matter. The interest was good, and the feeling was expressed that the community was in dire need of a proper
church. There followed a lengthy discussion as to where this
building should be located. There were several men who offered land, but it was finally decided that the most central location would be a corner of the Watley farm. A committee was

appointed to care for the pacing off and fencing of the area come fall. Another committee was assigned the task of log count. Throughout the winter months men and horses would strain and sweat in the task of getting the lumber transformed from tall standing timber in the hills to stripped logs lying in ever-increasing piles at the building site. It was the overseer's job to sort the logs and to make sure the secured number snaked in would be adequate for the building.

Everyone went home from the meeting with spirits lifted. Now they were finally getting someplace. The worship time would surely have a better chance to meet their needs. The church would be much bigger than the schoolhouse. It would have two side rooms. One where the children could profit from a Sunday school class, and a smaller one where fussing babies could be taken.

Wooden benches would be made that would meet the needs of full-grown men who had Sunday by Sunday been forced to curl their long frames into a desk created for a fifth grader. There would be an altar where people with needs could bow in prayer and a pulpit from which the Word of God could be proclaimed.

People began to visualize and dream of what it would be like when they had their own church.

The Reverend seemed to agree, though not enthuse, with the plan. It was fine with him as long as he was not called upon for some such task as log cutting. He was quick to inform the gentlemen of the great number of hours needed in his study for the purpose of preparing himself for his Sunday sermon.

The men were content to let him be. No one really felt the need for the Reverend's right arm in doing a task they had always handled with no problem.

After the crops had been harvested and the fall work completed, the men took to the wooded hills. Their own wood supply must be secured first, and they were in a hurry to complete the task so that they could start tallying up logs for the new church.

The winter wore on, and each day that was fit for man and

beast carried the sharp sound of the axes and the crashing of the large timbers. Gradually the piles of logs increased, and Clark, who was keeping the tally and overseeing the peeling, felt satisfaction in the progress they were making.

With the spring thaw, many piles of naked steaming poles lay in the warm spring sun. A day in May was set aside for the church raisin'. A church, being special, the men had contented themselves would take more than one day to see completion; but the first day would give them the sense of direction, the raw outline with which to work.

They met on the appointed day and the men set to work with a will. The ladies chatted and cooked and chased hungry children out of the food set aside for dinner. The building went well and as the tired farmers headed for home to their waiting chores, the walls of the church stood stout and strong. Those who could, would take the next day to work again on the building. The important thing now was to get the roof on, the windows in, and the door hung. The finishing on the inside would be done throughout the entire spring and summer as men could spare the time.

By fall their church stood tall, even bearing a spire that pointed to heaven. Only a bell was lacking, thought many of the more sentimental ladies. Only a bell.

To the east of the church a cemetery was carefully staked out. Marty wondered as she watched the men plotting the area if others around carried the same question in their hearts. Who would be the first to be laid to rest there?

She tried to brush aside the uncomfortable thought, but unconsciously her eyes travelled over her neighbors. She loved them. She would not wish to lose any of them. Then her eyes sought out her own family and she choked up a bit.

"I'm bein' silly," she scolded herself. "Our lives all be in God's hands. He'll do the choosin'."

She went to join Clark who was holding a squirming Ellie, wishing to be down to run with the rest of the small fry.

The dedication of the new church was set for the first Sunday in October. It was decided that they'd make a real celebration of it all and bring in a potluck meal.

The great day arrived. The wind was blowing, the sky overcast, making the day less than desired, but at least there was no rain falling. Marty was thankful for that.

She packed with care the food that she had prepared and made sure that her family was well bundled against the weather. Arnie was hard to corner long enough to be sure that he was properly buttoned and tied.

The crowd poured in, full of great expectation. They now had a church in which to worship. It would be so much easier to feel close to God.

They enjoyed singing lustily the familiar hymns. By now they knew fairly well some of the new songs that the Reverend had brought with him.

The prayer was long and elaborate. Marty found herself praying her own more simple one that met the need of her own heart.

Then they moved into the dedication service for the new building. Clark, Ben and Mr. Watley each had a part. Marty thought that it was beautiful, and her heart swelled with pride as she watched Clark participate.

"Now ya watch yer pa," her eyes told her youngsters. "See how straight he stands—how steady his voice—how proud he be to be a part of God's people. Watch yer pa."

The dedication came to a close and the morning sermon began.

"Oh, dear God, make it special. Make it a feedin' time," Marty prayed, but the dear Reverend hadn't gone far until she realized that she was going to again be disappointed. She finally let the anticipation drain from her and settled down to bear out the sermon in attentiveness rather than with understanding.

The Reverend, too, had felt that the sermon on such a splendid occasion should be special, so he had prepared an extra long one.

Children fidgeted, and one couldn't help but feel that the fathers felt a bit envious of the mothers who got to take them out.

At last the sermon ended and the congregation stood for

the closing hymn. The people filed from the building—the men to gather in small clusters, the children to stretch muscles cramped from so long a time unused, and women to put out the noonday meal.

It was a pleasant time spent together. The newlyweds accepted teasing good-naturedly, babies were passed around and exclaimed over, news from town and community was shared. It was a good day. Still Marty went away feeling disappointed. It hadn't been what she had hoped it would be. Something was definitely lacking. She pushed the thought aside, determined to talk about it with Clark later. Maybe he'd be able to put his finger on it.

# Chapter 34

# *Family*

A short note arrived from Tommie. It was the third time they had heard from him. Each time that news came Marty breathed a prayer of thanks that he was still safe. This letter stated that he was doing fine. He planned to stay where he was for the winter—working in a lumber mill. Thought he would push on again come spring. Maybe even to the coast. Hadn't had himself a look at the ocean yet. He sent his love.

He gave no return address and even the postage stamp was blurred, so they were none the wiser as to his whereabouts. They had hoped to respond by writing to let him know that they wished him well and hoped that he would soon be returning home.

Marty shared the letter at mealtime with all those about the table. Clark had read it previously but listened carefully as she read. She could see relief in his eyes. He thought highly of young Tom.

Time had erased much of the anxiety from the young Missie. She now seemed to think very little of the young man who had suddenly gone from her life—the man that she had childishly pledged herself to marry.

Marty looked about her table. How changed they all were from the time when Tom had left. She supposed that he had changed, too.

Nandry was now a young lady. She was still quiet, though always industrious. Marty had eventually given up trying to get close to her and accepted her as she was. "Bless her heart," thought Marty, "she's been worth her keep an' thet $10 over and over agin." Yet Marty was well aware that Nandry would likely be lost to them before long.

At least two of the neighborhood boys were busy studying Nandry. And, Marty observed, Nandry always looked back with flushed cheeks and an unusual twinkle in her eye.

Clae, too, was almost a young lady. She was near the end of her education in the one-room school, but not anywhere near the end of her hunger for knowledge. Marty and Clark had lain nights discussing her. Her burning desire was to become a teacher, and Clark felt that even though many dollars would be involved, Clae should be given the opportunity. Clae would have to go away for her schooling. Marty dreaded the thought.

Missie was eleven now—still a bundle of energy that was one minute a little girl and the next minute stretching toward womanhood. She loved school; in fact, Missie welcomed each new venture. She still did not like Willie LaHaye. But now she just ignored him.

Clare was nine. A bright boy who still preferred *doing* to learning; though there was nothing wrong with his ability in either area. He still mimicked Clark and watched carefully to see how his pa handled situations.

Arnie in turn followed Clare. Almost six, Arnie was going to be allowed to attend school this fall.

Three-year-old Ellie was a small bundle of brightness in everybody's life. Happy and playful, she darted among them like a small butterfly, enriching the lives of all whom she touched.

In the family cradle rested a new little head. Baby Luke had been added to the family. More than once Marty had sincerely thanked God for Nandry since the arrival of little Luke, for unlike her others, this baby was a fussy one, demanding attention just at the time when a mother was the busiest. Nandry did her best to comfort the unhappy child.

"My family," thought Marty, looking round the table. "My strange, wonderful family." Lest she become teary-eyed with emotion just thinking of each one, she herded her thoughts back to safer ground and went on with her meal. Clark rescued her.

"Saw Cam today."

"Did ya?"

"He had Rett with 'im. Do ya know thet thet boy can already handle a team. Should've see'd Cam. Proud as punch. Says Rett's gonna be the best horseman in these here parts. Might too. Seems to be a natural with animals."

"Isn't thet somethin'."

"Cam says he wouldn't be none surprised to see thet lad take 'im on the tamin' of a bear. Never says a word, but he seems to make the animals understand 'im.

"Mr. Cassidy says thet Cam never comes to town but he brings Rett either on the wagon beside 'im or up in front of 'im in the saddle."

Mr. Cassidy was the gentleman who had taken over the McDonald's store.

Clark seemed to be deep in thought for a moment.

"Funny thing. Cam's changed. Watchin' 'im move about town with his son I noticed a thoughtfulness 'bout 'im. He ain't thinkin' on Cam Marshall no more. I think others note it, too. Seem to have new respect fer 'im someway. Thought as I watched 'im leavin' town with thet boy up there beside 'im handlin' the reins, 'There goes a real man.' "

Marty nodded, her eyes clouding a bit, but mostly her thoughts were of Wanda and the happiness that she would feel in having given Cam a son that he could love and be proud of. She switched the subject.

"Did ya happen to see Mr. McDonald?"

"Yeah. Saw 'im sittin' on the bench out in front of the store with Ole Tom and Jake Feidler. Didn't talk to 'im more than a howdy."

"How's he seem?"

"Pretty good. I think thet he be right glad to be back."

Mrs. McDonald had passed away two years previously,

having never recovered from her stroke. Mr. McDonald had decided after her funeral to return East, but time had brought him West again.

"Jest didn't feel to home there," was the only explanation that he gave, so he took a room at Mrs. Keller's boardinghouse and spent his days chatting, whittling, and spitting tobacco juice out in front of his old store. Mr. Cassidy didn't seem to mind, though Mrs. Cassidy tired somewhat of scrubbing the steps.

Marty wondered what it would be like to go back East after having been gone so long. Her own pa was gone now and her ma lived alone. They kept in touch, though the letters were sometimes far apart. Marty did try to at least keep her posted on each new family member and to send her greetings at Christmastime.

No, she was sure that she wouldn't feel at home there anymore either.

She gently slapped Arnie's finger away from the butter and gave him a piece of buttered bread. The years had brought so many changes—most of them good ones.

# Chapter 35

# *Nandry*

Young Josh Coffins was the first to make a move in showing serious intention toward Nandry. Marty knew that it was bound to come. She favored it and deplored it at the same time.

Fall work was over again, leaving a young man time to think of things like courting. Josh approached Clark after church one Sunday to ask permission to call. Clark was not a dense man, but he did take pleasure in teasing.

"Sure thing, Josh. I'd be most happy to have ya drop by to see me. Reckon we could have us a quiet talk—like out in the barn where we'd not be interrupted by small fry and women."

Josh reddened and stammered as he endeavored to explain that that wasn't really what he had in mind. Clark laughed and slapped him on the back good-naturedly, and Josh realized that he'd been "had."

He laughed at the joke on himself and felt good within that this respected man of the community would trouble himself to tease him.

"Yer welcome to come," Clark said more seriously, "an' I promise ya not to be holdin' ya at the barn."

Josh grinned, muttered his thanks and walked off. The way had been cleared. Now to approach Nandry.

He found her sitting on the church steps, several youngsters in tow. Baby Luke was on her lap, pointing out horses and wagons with his usual "Wha' dat?"

Josh leaned carelessly on the handrailing. Nandry looked up and the color of her face deepened.

"Been talkin' to Clark." Previously Josh had always said Mr. Davis as he had been properly taught.

Nandry's eyes widened at his words as well as his deportment, for Josh seemed to evidence a kind of emotional swagger. She waited.

"He says it be fine with 'im if I come a callin'."

Nandry's color deepened still more. Still she said nothing.

"Be it okay with you?" There, the question was out. The ball was now handed to Nandry. There was no way that she could pretend not to understand his meaning. She flushed a deep red and studied the child on her lap. Minutes ticked by. It seemed an eternity to Josh who stood waiting, heart pounding and hands sweating.

"I reckon," finally came the soft answer and Josh's face broke into a relieved grin. He wanted to throw back his head and whoop, but something warned him that he'd better not do that.

"Thanks," he said to Nandry. The evenness of his voice surprised him. "Thanks. Next Wednesday then. I'll be lookin' forward to it," and then he was gone, suppressing the urge to run and leap the nearby pump.

Nandry buried her blushing face against the small Luke, her heart pounding in her ears. She had been hoping that it would be Josh. She had noticed Willis Aitkins looking at her, too, but she had really favored Josh. He had not even waited for the customary Saturday call. Usually when the young folks started to keep company, the calls were made on Saturday night. Only the very serious called on *both* Saturday and Wednesday, and Josh had said he'd see her Wednesday. Nandry hoped with all of her heart that Clark and Marty would approve. She wanted so much to do what would please them, but she realized that she also was feeling a strong tug toward Josh Coffins.

She lifted the small Luke and held him to her so closely

that he squirmed in protest.

"Oh, Lukey." She called him that only when she felt especially affectionate. "How can one feel so happy, an' sad, an' excited, an' scared all at one time?"

Luke didn't understand the question, but he reached out his baby hand to touch the tear that lay glistening on her cheek.

# Chapter 36

## *The Excitement of Christmas*

Another Christmas was drawing close, and as Marty made preparations she felt that this would be a very special Christmas. Never, over the last several Christmases, had Marty felt such intense excitement.

Baby Luke toddled about, a happy child, having finally outgrown his fussiness. Ellie was still a bundle of activity, but now small bits of the energy could already be channeled into helpful areas. Arnie, Clare, and Missie would enjoy the break from school and were already making plans for sliding on the creek's frozen surface and sledding down its banks. The most important ingredient adding to the extra excitement was that Clae would be home. Clae, their little would-be-teacher—Marty could hardly wait.

Clae's letters were filled with excitement about what she was learning, who she was meeting, but most important, how much she was missing them all.

Marty felt that the days would never pass quickly enough until the time came for Clark to meet her in town.

She fussed over all of Clae's favorite dishes, made sure that Nandry had the shared room prepared, and coaxed the younger children to feel the same excitement that she felt. There would be another *first* at their Christmas table as well. Josh Coffins, Nandry's promised fiancé, would be joining them.

Marty shared in the joy of the young couple, but she dreaded the thought of losing her Nandry.

A spring wedding was planned and as soon as the rush of Christmas was put aside, Nandry and Marty would get down to the serious business of preparing the bridal dowry.

Nandry seemed very happy, and Marty had for some months been giving her the egg money so that she would have something with which to buy the little "extras."

But first she would feast upon Christmas.

Clark chose the tree and the evergreen boughs that would form their traditional wreaths.

This year a turkey would not be purchased as Nandry had added a half-dozen turkeys to her chicken pens.

A fine young gobbler was chosen to honor the Christmas dinner table and was getting extra daily care and attention from Nandry.

Pies, tarts, and cookies, along with loaf cakes, lined the shelves in the pantry.

Marty had been to town for her shopping, and gifts laid wrapped beside her chest of drawers or hidden beneath her bed to supply socks for Christmas morning.

On the day that Clae was to arrive, both Nandry and Marty felt almost too excited to work. Marty was glad that she had much to do to help the time go faster. Still it seemed that the clock would never get around to the time when they were expected home.

At last it came and Marty heard Ole Bob's sharp bark, and the happy shouts of children.

Missie was the first one in.

"Guess who we found?" she teased.

"Where did you come from?" asked Marty.

"Pa came round by the school to give us a ride, too, seeing it was closin' time."

They all came tramping in then, Clark bringing up the rear, carrying Clae's suitcase and a large bag.

Marty pulled the girl into her arms.

"Oh, Clae, jest look at ya. Why ya've gone and plumb growed up on us since ya been away."

Clae hugged her in return.

"Oh, it's so good to be home. I could hardly wait."

She went from Marty to her sister and then to Ellie and Luke, hugging each one in turn, and exclaiming over how the youngsters had all grown, and making Nandry's cheeks flush red with teasing her about her Josh.

The whole cabin took on an atmosphere of celebration, and the chattering was both confusing and near deafening.

"I be thinkin'," said Clark, setting down the suitcase and the bundle, "thet we be needin' a bigger house."

Marty just smiled. They were hard put for space at times; she knew that. Again she was having to put up with a crib in her bedroom, and the three girls who shared one room barely had room to turn around.

They were crowded, but they were happy. The conversation did not lessen as the evening wore on. There were so many things for Clae to tell, to describe. There were so many questions for the others to ask.

After the young had been put to bed, with the promise of full socks in the morning, Marty, Nandry, and Clae still talked on. Clark listened and added his occasional comment.

"When's the day for your wedding?" Clae asked Nandry, and Marty noticed Clae's careful speech.

"The last o' May. We wanted to wait 'til ya'd be home. You're to be my maid o' honor, ya know."

"I hoped that I would. Where are you going to live?"

"There's a small cabin on the Coffins' farm. The people who usta farm it lived in it. The Coffins built a bigger one when they came. We'll use the little 'un fer now."

"You must be excited?"

"I am," said Nandry and her face verified it. "It's a funny feelin'. I want so much fer time to go quickly, yet I hate it at the same time."

"Meanin'?" Clae forgot herself for the moment and used a familiar expression.

"This house—the kids—I really hate to leave the kids."

It was the first time that Marty had ever heard Nandry give anyone a glimpse into how she felt. It made her feel closer to the girl.

"You won't be too far away," said Clae. She shook her

head. "No one will ever know how homesick I was at first. I thought I'd just die if I didn't get home. I thought that I'd just never make it—but I did. I reminded myself of the money paid for my schooling—the faith that people had in me—and—and I remembered Ma, too. Sometimes I think about Ma, about how proud she'd be, how happy that we got a chance."

Marty remembered too.

"She'd be happy for both of us," Clae went on—"for me being a teacher, for you marrying Josh. It sort of gives it extra meaning, remembering Ma."

It was the first time that the girls had ever talked to her about their mother. Marty spoke softly.

"Yer ma would be very proud. She wanted so much thet ya both make good, an' ya have, both of ya, an' I'm proud, too."

Clae put her arms around Marty's neck and gave her an affectionate squeeze.

"And we know why," she said. "We never say much maybe—not as much as we should, but we know why we've made good. Thank you—thank you so much. I do love you and I'll never forget—never."

Nandry nodded her head in agreement but said nothing.

## Chapter 37

# *Christmas Dinner*

The household was awakened early the next morning by Arnie's squeals of delight. Clare's voice soon joined his and then a general hub-bub followed. Marty pulled herself out of bed and slipped into her house-socks and robe. Clark was already on his feet, tucking his shirt into his trousers. They entered the sitting room together and watched the excited children. Nandry came in carrying the awakened Luke, and Ellie danced round the room waving her arms excitedly. So far, she had been caught up in Arnie and Clare's yelling and had not even thought to check out what her own stocking might hold.

Luke quickly dismissed the silly antics of his older kin and stood transfixed, gazing at the glittering tree in the corner that had sprung up from somewhere during the night.

Missie emerged rubbing her sleepy eyes.

"It's not even five o'clock," she said in disbelief. "Ya usta make me wait."

"They'd waited, too, iffen I'd had enythin' to do with it," responded Clark, but Marty noticed that he seemed to be enjoying the whole, wild uproar.

Eventually things began to simmer down, the fire was kindled in the kitchen stove and the kettle put on to boil. The fireplace was replenished and coaxed to flame.

The children's roar simmered to an excited hum, and the adults took advantage of the near quiet to exchange their gifts. Clae had somehow managed to bring a small gift for each of them. Marty knew that she did not have much extra spending money and appreciated her gift the more for it. What Clae had lacked in shekels she had supplied with creativity, and her sewing skills had come to the fore. Luke had received a stuffed teddy bear; Ellie, a pint-sized apron complete with pocket; Arnie and Clare, checkered man-sized handkerchiefs. For Missie there was a lace-trimmed bonnet, and for Nandry a carefully embroidered pair of pillowcases for her hopechest. Marty unwrapped her gift to see the most beautiful lace handkerchief that she had ever seen, but the note that accompanied it was what made Marty cry, for it bore the simple words, "To Mother, with love, Clae." None of her children had ever called her Mother, and it seemed appropriate for this "special" child to use the name.

Clark's gift, too, carried sentiment, and he slipped the card that accompanied it into Marty's hand, knowing that it would bring her pleasure. The card read, "Thanks for being a true pa. Love, Clae."

Marty tried to blink away the happiness that was showing in her eyes and exclaimed over the new woolen mittens that Clark was proudly trying on.

Nandry too had surprises for them. She had made picture books for all of the younger children, gluing the newspaper and calendar pictures that she had gathered onto pieces of cloth. Missie received new hair ribbons—her sense of self-esteem ever needing bolstering by new ribbons. Marty got a little wooden box to hold her many and varied recipes that were forever flooding over in the drawer space where she kept them. Clark received a hand-made cover for his well-worn family Bible.

Marty and Clark passed 'round their presents and watched with pleasure the shining eyes of the recipients.

The clutter was cleared away, the cherished gifts put carefully in their new places of belonging, and the day proceeded, the excitement spilling over into every area.

After breakfast Clare and Arnie were allowed to go out to try the new sled that Clark had made them. Ellie went, apron-clad, to play with her tiny new dishes, and Luke was put back to bed to catch up on some of the sleep he had been denied.

Missie, feeling quite grown-up, went with the ladies to the kitchen, where she followed orders in helping to prepare the Christmas dinner.

Josh arrived earlier than expected. He just didn't seem to be able to stay away. He shyly but eagerly offered Nandry his gift. It was a new lamp to be used in their home. Marty had never seen a prettier one. A soft cluster of roses was painted on the bowl in reds and pinks, and the shade was generously trimmed with gold. What Nandry presented to Josh, the family did not get to see, but Marty had her suspicions that it was a mustache cup—for Josh was nursing a mustache that he hoped to have full and well-groomed by his wedding day, making him feel more like a man.

They roasted chestnuts at the fire and sniffed hungrily at the cooking odors coming from the kitchen. Just before the meal was set on the table, the family gathered for the reading of the Christmas story. Even Luke, from his spot on Nandry's knee, appeared to listen. Marty looked 'round the room at all the happy faces and her heart filled up with praise. She slipped her hand into Clark's during his prayer and he pressed her fingers firmly.

Just as the chairs were being placed around the table, Ole Bob began to bark. It was unusual to have uninvited guests on Christmas Day, and Marty felt her heart flutter, hoping that nothing was wrong. She followed Clark to the door, almost afraid to look out.

She could hear the footsteps approaching the door and with barely a knock the door pushed open.

"Tommie," was all she could say.

"Tommie," echoed Clark, equally incredulous. "Good to see ya, boy," he said, greeting the young man with a bear hug.

Then it was Marty's turn—then greetings all round, excitedly and with great gusto.

"Jest a minute," Tommie said holding up his hand. "I got somethin' to show ya."

He was gone, but soon back, his arm around a small, blond-haired girl who came forward shyly.

"My wife," he said with pride; "my wife, Fran."

"Oh, Tommie," said Marty. "Tommie, when did ya

marry? Why didn't ya write?"

Tommie laughed joyously. "Five months ago now. I wanted to surprise ya. Isn't she somethin'?" He looked at her again and his arm tightened. Fran smiled—beginning to cope with her feeling of being overwhelmed.

"I'm pleased to meet ya all," she said, putting out one small hand to Clark and then Marty.

Marty stepped forward to give her a welcoming embrace.

"An' we are jest so glad to meet you. Won't ya come in? Take off yer coats. We are jest sittin' down, an' we are so pleased to have ya join us."

"No, no," said Tom, "we haven't been home yet. We must run, but I did want ya to meet her, first off. Ma would never fergive me iffen I stopped here to eat Christmas dinner."

That was true, Marty knew, but there was so much that she wanted to talk about.

"Oh, it's gonna be so hard to let ya go now. I've a million questions."

"They'll keep," said Tommie. "We'll be around. I decided thet I'd take up thet piece of land o' mine. See iffen I can make a farm outta it. Fran's ma and pa owned a store out West. Now there's a switch, huh?" he winked; "long comes a guy, marries yer daughter, an' takes her *East*."

"Oh, Tommie! I hope thet you'll be so happy."

"We already are," Tommie assured her, and his eyes said that it was true.

They bid their good-byes and promised to be back soon for a nice, long visit.

The family returned to their Christmas dinner.

"Well, this has truly been some day." Marty expressed the feelings of them all.

They bowed their heads and Clark's deep voice spoke reverently to their Father, thanking Him for the many blessings that life held, and especially for Tommie, a son come home and the joy that it would bring to the Graham household.

Marty wondered about the pretty Owahteeka. Had she found happiness with her Running Deer? Marty truly hoped so.

# Chapter 38

## *Tryin' Agin*

The people of the community reluctantly admitted to themselves and finally to one another that the highly trained Reverend Watson was just not fitting in to their community and meeting the needs of the congregation.

Now that they had admitted it, they wondered why it had taken them so long to bring it to the fore. What to do about the problem became the next question, and it was one that did not seem to have an easy answer.

A committee was picked in due course and much to Marty's chagrin, Clark was named as chairman. A meeting was called at which time the men hoped to be able to discuss quite openly with the Reverend Watson how the people felt.

The Reverend showed no surprise at being asked to meet with the men, but the meeting itself had its touchy moments. It appeared that the Reverend thought the meeting had been called to offer him commendations, and perhaps to even suggest an increase in his rather meager, to his standards at any rate, salary.

He was taken aback when the meeting took a different turn.

It came to light that the Reverend was not only educated himself but was also using the brains of other highly trained theologians. Much of his sermon material was copied directly from one textbook or another.

The good Reverend found it hard to believe that anyone could be so unappreciative as to not highly favor his intellectually charged sermons. He had had no idea that the people of the area were so bereft of learning and so insensitive to spiritual enlightenment. He would do better. He knew of a great scholar whose books had just been made available, and though they were full of exceptional material, they were written in the "easy language of the layman." He'd send for a couple. He was sure that the people would find encouragement and religious sustenance in the works of this great man.

It was with difficulty that the committee, Clark in particular, convinced the Reverend that what they were there to say was that they wished him to end his service to them as their minister.

Clark said it thus, "Reverend, we realize thet ya are a very learned man, an' we realize thet we be a mite slow. We wouldn't want to hold ya back from preachin' to those who could understand and appreciate yer great skills, so we are releasin' ya to go back to wherever ya wish to go, an' at such time as ya are first able to make the arrangement."

The Reverend sputtered. "Are you saying, gentlemen," he finally choked, "are you saying that my service has been terminated?"

"Shucks, no," put in the elder Coffins, who was also a committee member, "not terminated, jest excused."

So they excused the parson, gave him a going away purse, wished him well, and got on with the job of selecting a new minister. This time Mr. Wilbur Whittle was not asked to serve as correspondent.

The parson had no more than packed his bags and left the area than the people had a reason to wish him back. As yet the cemetery beside the little church stood empty of markers. They all knew that it could not always be so, and the unasked question often hung in the air—who? Who would be the person who would cause the ground to be first broken in order that they might be laid to rest?

Unconsciously they observed their neighbors. Grandpa

Stern was well on in years and seemed to be failing. Mrs. LaHaye had never really recovered her full health. One of the Coffin girls seemed very delicate and was always down with one sickness or another. Her parents didn't even allow her to go to school. Mrs. Vickers showed signs of high blood pressure, and some feared that she'd talk herself right into an early grave. But when it happened—it was none of these, and the whole community was shaken by the suddenness and the sadness of it all.

It was Tessie. It took some while to accept. Tessie had always seemed like such a strong, healthy girl, and the community folk were pleased when the evidence showed that she was going to make her schoolteacher husband a father. As for Mr. Whittle himself, his bowler hat had never been dusted more frequently, his giant mustache been trimmed with more care, nor his spats whitened with such vigor. He was well pleased with himself. To have a young and attractive wife who idolized him was a wonder in itself, and to be about to become a father was hardly bearable for its magnitude. Mr. Whittle was on cloud nine. The big boys teased that his voice was now always squeaking with excitement, but Mr. Whittle did not seem to notice.

The great day came and the doctor was duly sent for. With tired eyes and a heavy heart, he left the next morning. Both Tessie and her baby boy had died during the night. The news shook the whole community. The neighbors responded, the grave was dug in the new cemetery, the pine box formed and carefully draped, the bodies prepared for burial. Through it all Mr. Wilbur Whittle moved as one in a daze. It was beyond his comprehension, this great loss. He could never believe nor accept it. In the absence of a parson, Mr. Whittle did have presence of mind enough to ask Clark if he'd read the scripture and say the words. Clark accepted.

The day of the funeral was a cold, dreary day. The pine box was lowered, the earth heaped upon it.

Marty stood gazing at the fresh grave that held a young mother with a baby boy in her arms. "It's no longer virgin— this cemetery. From now on it will be grave added to grave."

Time and again the earth would be opened up and asked to receive a new burden.

"Oh, Tessie," Marty cried inwardly, "who would have thought that it would be you! Life be full of the unexpected."

Classes were cancelled until further notice, but Mr. Whittle never did get around to resuming them, so school for that term ended in April. And toward the end of May, when the roses were beginning to bloom and the birds were rebuilding their nests, Mr. Whittle took a bouquet of wild flowers and placed it on the new mound of earth. Then dusting his bowler hat, he picked up his suitcases and returned to the East.

# Chapter 39

# *Josh and Nandry*

The Parson's leaving had two other members of the congregation feeling concern. Josh and Nandry became worried about what it would do to their wedding plans. Clark perceived what they must be thinking and did some inquiring on his own.

He discovered a parson two towns away and made arrangements for the man to be at their community church on the day that had been set for the wedding.

When he felt quite confident that nothing would happen to put a hitch in the plans, he broke the news to Josh and Nandry.

"This here weddin' ya been a plannin'—ya changed yer minds 'bout it?"

"Oh, no," Nandry said, looking to Josh for support.

"Gonna be a bit tricky without a preacher."

Josh agreed sullenly, and Nandry looked about to cry, a thing that Nandry had never been known to do.

"Jest so happened," Clark went on hurriedly, the teasing now gone from his voice, "thet I heerd of a man within ridin' distance who also happens to be a church-recognized parson."

The two faces focused intently on his.

"Where?" asked Josh. "Do ya think we could go to 'im?"

"Reckon there ain't much need fer thet," Clark said lazily.

"He said thet he'd be happy to come on over here."

Nandry had sat silently taking it all in, but rose with a sudden whoop.

"Are ya sayin' thet ya found us a parson?" she cried.

Clark grinned. "Thet's 'bout it, I guess."

"Oh, bless ya!" Nandry squealed. She was about ready to throw her arms around Clark, then turned quickly to embrace Josh instead. Josh didn't mind.

Marty smiled. "Nandry still has never been able to see him as a father," she thought. "He's always been 'the man.' 'The man' thet she felt no right to love an' yet couldn't help lovin'."

Her attention was drawn back to the happy couple and the grinning Clark.

"When?" said Nandry. "When can he come?"

"Well, I thought as how you'd set yer mind on May twenty-eighth."

"We did—we have. Ya mean we can have the weddin' jest as we planned—in the church—with our friends?"

"Yup—jest as planned."

"Oh, glory!" said Nandry. "He does answer."

The two left for a walk in the garden to share their moment of happiness and finalize their plans.

"Well," said Marty, her own happiness spilling over, "how did ya ever manage this bit of magic?"

"Didn't take no magic," Clark answered; "jest money."

The much-planned-for wedding was held as scheduled. The hired parson did a commendable job of reading the vows and instructing the bride and groom.

Nandry was radiant in her bridal gown, and Clae looked almost as pretty as she stood beside her sister.

Josh's younger brother, Joe, stood with him. It was a beautiful wedding full of meaning and promise, and when the guests turned from the ceremony to the bridal supper, there was much laughter and good-natured banter.

"Here ya are," Todd Stern said to Clark, "hardly dry behind the ears yet, an' already givin' a girl away."

Clark looked at his young Missie who was growing up all too quickly.

"An' 'fore I know it," he said quietly, "I'll be losin' thet one, too."

Todd sobered, feeling what Clark was feeling.

"Seems like yesterday I had 'em stumblin' round under my feet," he said, "an' here I am a grandpa. Sometimes wisht thet time had a tail, so's we could grab ahold an' slow it down some."

Throughout the summer months the church was without a pastor, but it did not alarm the people of the area to be left with a vacant pulpit. They were sure that in God's good time He would supply the right man.

The school, too, now was empty and a meeting of the governing board resulted in Clae being asked to take the classes come fall. Clae could hardly believe her good fortune. Here she was, newly returned from her teacher-training and already a school was promised to her, and her home school at that. Along with the excitement, there was mingled sorrow. The community still ached and prayed for Mr. Wilbur Whittle.

Marty, too, was excited about Clae's new job.

"It will be so good to have ya home agin. We missed ya so."

"You spoil me," said Clae. "In a lot of ways I would love to be home—but—well—I've a notion that I sort of want to be on my own. I really want to set up housekeeping in the teacherage. There are still dishes and everything there, and Mrs. LaHaye told me that I could just move in and make use of them if I'd like. I'd really love to. Besides, I'm doing some studies by mail and I'll truly need the quiet if I am to complete the course in the time allowed."

Marty was disappointed, but after a long discussion with Clark she reluctantly gave in. It wasn't like Clae would be off on her own. She would be, after all, just down the road and over the hill.

It was agreed that Clae would move in with Missie for the summer months to fill in some of the emptiness left by Nandry's departure. Then before the fall classes were to begin she'd move her belongings into the teacherage and set up housekeeping on her own.

Leads were followed up concerning a new minister. Possibilities arose, were investigated and discarded. Not that the searching committee was so hard to please; but few parsons were available, and those who were were generally found to wish a larger parish, or one that offered more amenities.

Toward fall Ben heard of a young man through Mr. Cassidy.

"He's from my former hometown," said the store manager. "Young fella—not too much book learnin'—did get some trainin' but hasn't been on to seminary in the East like he's a aimin' to. Got lots of spunk, an' sure does study out of the Good Book—honest an' hard workin', but green."

"We don't mind greenness none," Ben offered. "We's all pretty green ourselves; maybe we could learn together."

A two-man delegation left on horseback to see if they could track down the young man. It was eight days before they were home again, but when they returned they had good news.

They had located the man and he was eager to obtain a church. He still hoped to advance his education; but if they'd take him as he was, he'd do his best to serve them. They had agreed.

Pastor Joseph Berwick arrived on the fifth of September, the same day that Miss Clae Larson began her first classes in the country school. He was not to have his first sermon until the following Sunday, but he wished to call on his parishioners in the interim time.

He boarded with the Watleys and when Mrs. Watley beheld the tall good-looking young man, she scrutinized him thoroughly and then turned to her two daughters with a twinkle in her eyes. She gave the girls a sly wink and nodded the parson into the parlor where tea was served. "Surely this time," she sighed.

Parson Berwick was not content to sit and sip tea, and before the dust of his last trail had had a chance to settle, he was off again to meet the inhabitants of the area whom he saw as members of his flock.

He was not above lending a helping hand either and spent some time cutting wood for the Widow Rider, helped pound a fencepost that Jason Stern was placing, and forked hay along with the Graham boys.

Gradually he worked his way toward the schoolhouse, and on Thursday around four o'clock he paid a call on the local teacher.

Clae was not prepared for his coming, and was down on her knees in her neglected flower bed, cleaning out the weeds that had been left to grow where they wist over the summer. Her hair was pulled back with a ribbon and her slim hands were dirtied with soil.

She looked up in surprise at the approaching stranger. A streak of dirt across her nose gave her an innocent little-girl look.

The new parson dismounted and presented himself in a courteous manner.

"I'm Parson Berwick," he said politely. "Is your father at home?"

Clae just shook her head speechlessly, trying to sort out who he might mean by her father, and where she should tell him that he could be located.

"Your mother?"

"No—no one—I'm—" she changed her course; "you meaning the Davises?" she asked; "or the Larsons?"

It was the parson's turn to look confused. "I'm meaning the teacher," he said, "whoever he is. I haven't yet heard his name."

"There is no *he*."

"I beg your pardon."

"The teacher—he's—he's gone," Clae stumbled. "He doesn't live here anymore."

"I'm sorry," said the parson. "I understood that they were still having classes."

"They are—we are," Clae quickly amended.

"Are you one of the pupils?"

Clae stood up to her full height, which still didn't make much of an impression against the parson's tall frame.

"*I*," she emphasized the word, "am the teacher."

"The teacher!" he reddened. "Oh, my goodness!" he exclaimed. "Then I guess that I must want to see you instead of your father. I mean—I didn't really come to see him. I came to see the teacher."

After a pause, "Let's start all over, shall we?"

He stepped back, then stepped forward again with an impish smile.

"Hello there," he said, "I'm Pastor Berwick, new to your area and I'm endeavoring to call on each of my parishioners. I understand that you are the new schoolteacher hereabouts."

Clae looked down at her grubby hand, but the pastor did not hesitate. He reached for it and Clae felt her hand held in a firm handshake.

"I'm sorry," she stammered looking from him to her earth-covered hands.

"You've got dirt on your nose, too," he said with a smile.

"Oh, my!" said Clae, embarrassed. She reached up to rub at the suspected spot but only made it worse.

He laughed, and withdrawing a clean handkerchief, he stepped forward and wiped the smudge from her face.

Clae held her breath. Her throat felt tight and her heart pounded. She wondered if the parson heard it, too.

He stepped back and put his handkerchief neatly back in his pocket.

"As I said, I'm calling on my parishioners. Can I expect to see you in church on Sunday?"

"Oh, yes," whispered Clae, and blushed at her foolishness.

"And you really are the schoolteacher?"

She nodded.

"Sure didn't have teachers like that when I went to school."

She caught the twinkle in his eye, and her color deepened.

"I'll see you Sunday."

She nodded dumbly.

He mounted his horse and was about to move on, then stopped and turned to her.

"You didn't give me your name."

"Clae—Clae Larson."

"*Miss* Clae Larson?"

"Miss Clae Larson."

"How do you spell that? Clae. I've never heard that name before."

Clae spelled it. She hoped that it was right.

"Clae," he said; "that's unusual. I'll see you Sunday, Miss Larson."

She watched him ride away.

So it was that Clae met the new preacher, and so it was that she had problems with her concentration. Right from the very first she had trouble focusing her attention on the sermon rather than the man—but she never missed a Sunday.

## Chapter 40

# *Parson Joe*

The new parson, who was soon known as Parson Joe, was quick in establishing his place in the community. His willingness to lend a hand endeared him to the farmers.

"Not afraid to dirty his hands, thet one."

"No—nor to bend his back."

But the real reason for their nod of approval was the Sunday services. The parson made a list of all of the hymns that the congregation knew by heart, and these were sung heartily on Sundays. Occasionally new hymns were added by writing the words on a chalkboard borrowed from the school.

His prayers were not just wordy but full of sincerity, and his sermons were the highlight of the whole service. Simple straightforward messages, brought right from the Bible, gave the people a real sense of being nourished.

Even the youngsters began to take notice, and young Clint Graham surprised his folks by announcing that he had decided to go into the ministry.

Only Mrs. Watley was disappointed in the new parson— and that had nothing whatever to do with his Sunday sermons. She was beside herself to discover ways to make him pay more attention to one of her daughters—which one he chose, she didn't care, but the man seemed oblivious to either of them.

The congregation grew both numerically and spiritually. Willie LaHaye never missed a Sunday, and even Zeke LaHaye put aside an occasional Sunday morning for worship. Some felt that the loss of Tessie had softened the man somewhat. Marty noticed on more than one occasion his eyes on the silent mound across the yard. A carefully worked cross had appeared at the grave, bearing the words, "Tessie LaHaye Whittle and Baby Boy. May their rest be peaceful and never alone."

The parson called on his people more than for Sunday dinner, and wherever he went he was welcomed.

Claude Graham was heard remarking to his twin brother, Lem, "The reason thet he fits here so well is thet he don't know nothin' from them books neither."

To which Lem replied, "Don't let him fool ya. He's got a lot more of a load there then he's throwin' out each Sunday. No use forkin' a whole haystack to growin' calves."

As for Clae, she felt in a befuddled state. To get her mind off her confusion, she worked every spare minute on her education by mail. The course that could have taken until the next summer was completed by Christmas.

The parson was always friendly to her, but so he was with each member of his congregation. Still Clae couldn't stop the ridiculous skipping of her heart, the hoping that perhaps, just perhaps, he had noticed her and he was maybe just a bit more attentive to her than to some of the other girls. At times she despaired, at times she dreamed—if only—if only—and then on Easter Sunday morning following an inspirational service, the young parson held her hand just a bit longer as she left the church. She was the last one leaving, having stopped to gather her chalkboard.

"Good morning, Miss Larson." He smiled, and then he whispered, "I do wish that you didn't live alone. How in the world is a gentleman to call?"

Clae caught her breath.

She allowed herself what she hoped was a decent amount of time and then moved back home with the Davises.

# Chapter 41

## *The New House*

Clark and Marty sat enjoying a second cup of coffee. It seemed good just to sit and chat for a while. They so rarely had the opportunity.

"Looks as though we got us a real growin' church," said Clark.

"Yeah, it's so good to see folks comin' out."

"Thet wasn't what I was meanin'."

"Then what was ya meanin'?"

"I noticed thet Nandry an' Tommie's Fran are both in the family way."

Marty smiled. She had noticed it, too.

"Speakin' of growin'," Clark said after a silence. "I'm a thinkin' thet we've put it off fer too long."

"Meanin'?"

"This house—it's way too small. Shoulda built another ages ago."

"Seems a strange thing to be thinkin' on now. Notice who's around—jest you an' me an' little Luke. Soon he'll be off, too."

"Yeah," said Clark, "but they come home agin, an' when they do they don't usually come alone—iffen you've noticed."

Marty thought of Nandry and Josh and their coming baby. She also thought of Clae and the young parson. Even Missie was quickly growing up, and before long she would be entertaining callers.

"Maybe yer right," she said; "maybe we do need a bigger house. It's jest thet it seems so quiet-like when they're off to school."

"I think I'll spend me the winter hauling logs. This here new house—I been thinkin' on it a lot. Not gonna be a log one. Gonna be board—nice board."

"Thet'll cost a fortune."

"Not really. There's a mill over cros't the crik now. I can trade my logs in on lumber. Been a thinkin' on the layout, too. How ya feel 'bout an upstairs—not a loft but a real upstairs— with steps a goin' up—not a ladder—like them fancy houses back East?"

Marty caught her breath.

"Seems to me ya got pretty big dreams."

"Maybe—maybe I have, but I want you to do a little dreamin', too. I want this house to have what ya be a wantin'. More windows, closets fer clothes stead of pegs—whatever ya be a wantin'. Ya do some dreamin' an' write yer plans down on paper. We'll see iffen we can't make some dreams come true."

Marty felt that it was all too much.

"When, Clark?"

"Not next year—I don't s'pose. Gonna take a long while to git all those logs, but the year after—should be able to do it by then fer sure."

"Sounds—sounds—like a fairy tale," Marty finished, finally accepting the fact that it really could happen.

Clark grinned and stood up. He reached out and touched her hair.

"Did I ever tell ya that I love ya, Mrs. Davis?"

"I've heard it afore," said Marty, "but it bears repeatin' now an' then."

He put a finger under her chin and tipped her face, then leaned to plant a kiss on her nose.

"By the way," he said, "thet's mighty good coffee."

# Chapter 42

## *Life Moves On*

Missie was in her last year at the local school, and as her school days ended, Luke's would begin. Clae had promised the school one more term and then it was hoped that Missie would take over, for she, too, had decided to get her teacher's training.

Clae lived back at the Davises, and it was plain to see that her heart was not totally in her teaching. Marty decided that she would make a fine parson's wife. Though the Davis household got a lion's share of the young parson's calls, he did not neglect the rest of his parishioners. Only a few of the neighborhood young ladies felt any disturbance at the frequency of his calls on the Davises.

Marty dreaded the thought of Missie going away to school. Somehow it seemed even harder than it had been to let Clae go. For one thing, Missie was younger than Clae had been, having started school at six, where Clae had been older and even with doubling up on a lot of her grades, she was older when she finished.

Clark spent the winter months hauling logs to the mill across the creek. He was well pleased with the progress he was making and could see no problem with building the promised new house by the next year.

Nandry's baby girl had arrived. They named her Tina

Martha after her *two* maternal grandmothers, Nandry said, and Marty felt her eyes mist.

Fran and Tommie's baby arrived about the same time. A solid boy, whom they named Ben.

Sally Anne gave birth to her third child, but little Emily lived only three days, and a tiny fresh mound was made in the cemetery by the church.

Rett Marshall was now handling a team of horses 'most as good as a grown man. He loved creatures, tame or wild, and even had a young jackrabbit for a pet. A strange boy, people were saying, but now there was admiration in their voices.

Marty remembered the conversation that she had overheard long ago between Mrs. Vickers and the doctor.

"I often wonder, Doctor, how a man feels when he sees what his skill has done. Do ya ever wish thet maybe ya hadn't—well—hadn't fought quite so hard-like?"

The doctor had looked at her evenly, sternly.

"Oh, course not," he finally answered. "I didn't make that life—the Creator did—and when He made it, I expect that He had good reason for doing as He did—and what that reason is, is His business."

Marty thought of this each time that she watched the boy whistle a bird down or make friends with a prairie dog. She thought of it, too, when she saw the love in Wanda's eyes or heard Cam's proud boasting.

The LaHaye farmstead didn't resemble anything that had ever belonged to Jedd Larson. Zeke LaHaye was a good farmer who knew land well. Under his care the fields produced and the farm prospered. New buildings were erected and a new well was dug. Neat rows of fencing encircled the holdings. Still, for all of the prosperity of the land, Mrs. LaHaye remained in poor health. Nathan married a girl from town and moved her into the big house with the family. She was a pleasant girl and was able to take over much of the care of the home and was a great source of comfort to the senior Mrs. LaHaye.

All around her, Marty saw change. New neighbors moved in. There was very little farmland now that wasn't taken. New buildings sprang up in town, almost overnight it seemed, as new businesses were added. The town had even built a church of its own and had brought in a parson to care for the people. There was a sheriff's office and a bank for those who needed them. All this nearby, and in their small community they felt almost self-sufficient.

They had their church, they had their school, they even had a doctor they could call for. Marty didn't feel much like a pioneer anymore.

The next summer saw Clae and the young parson joined together in marriage. Instead of bringing in a parson to do the honors, the young couple went out. Parson Joe was anxious to introduce Clae to his family and also eager to have his former pastor and dear friend perform the ceremony. The Davises hated to miss the event but made plans instead for a supper to honor the couple upon their return.

A daily stage now ran between the local towns, and Clae and her bridegroom were able to travel by stage rather than on horseback.

The school board had agreed to rent them the teacherage for a modest amount, as Missie, upon commencing her duties, preferred to live at home.

# Chapter 43

## *Learnin' the Cost*

In spite of a bad accident with an axe, Clark met his log quota the following winter.

He had been cutting logs alone on the hillside when the axe blade glazed off a knot and spun sideways slicing deeply into his foot. He had bound his foot as best as he could, packing moss against it and tying it tightly with a strip of his shirt. He was trying to make it home on one of his new work horses, Prince, when Tom Graham found him.

Prince was not used to being ridden, and Clark had his hands full trying to handle the excited horse in his weakened condition. He lost a lot of blood and was quite content to be helped from the skitterish horse to Tom's wagon box where he could lie down.

Tom pressed the horses forward in an effort to get Clark home as quickly as possible. He threw the harnesses on the fence and took his own horse, Dixie, to go for the Doc. Dixie was used to being ridden bareback.

Marty nearly fainted at the sight of Clark. He tried to assure her that he would be fine, but his face was so white and his hands so shaky that she wasn't convinced. Marty got him to bed where she fussed and fretted over him, hardly knowing what should be done.

"If ya see no fresh blood," Tom had admonished, "best ya leave thet foot alone 'til the Doc gits here."

Marty studied the foot for signs of fresh blood, but thankfully none seemed to appear.

Being a woman, her thoughts went to food.

"Could ya eat a little broth iffen I fixed it? Yer gonna need yer strength, ya know."

It didn't seem to appeal much to Clark, but he shook his head in the affirmative, then cautioned, "Not too hot—jest warm."

Marty complied. The hours until the doctor came seemed endless, but at last Marty heard a horse approaching. She stayed out of the room while the doctor cleaned and sutured the cut. A couple of times she heard Clark groan, and her knees nearly buckled beneath her.

"And you," the doctor caught her by surprise, "you are most as white as he is. You best sit you down and have a cup of hot, weak tea with some honey in it."

"Gonna take him awhile but he'll be fine. He's young and tough. He'll make it. Your big job is going to be to keep him off the foot until it has a chance to heal proper-like. Have a notion that your job won't be an easy one. Can't you put him to mending or piecing a quilt?"

There was humor in the doctor's eyes and Marty laughed outright. The thought of Clark sitting contentedly with a little needle in his big working hand, matching dainty pieces for quilting, was just too much.

In spite of the deepness of the cut and the loss of blood involved, the foot healed neatly and quickly. Clare and Arnie took over the chores and were quite able to handle them.

Soon, Marty's biggest problem was to keep Clark down as the doctor had ordered. He chaffed at not being able to be up and busy as he was used to being.

Parson Joe came as often as he could for a game of checkers. He usually brought Clae along. Other neighbors dropped in now and then. They informed him that the logs that had already been felled would be hauled to the mill before spring thaw, just as he had planned. Clark accepted their kindness with deep appreciation.

Missie brought home books for him to read, which helped him pass many hours.

Finally, the long ordeal was over and Doc declared the foot well enough to be stepped on again. Clark hobbled, but at least he was again on his feet—a fact that each member of the household was truly thankful for. He never did completely lose his limp, and Marty noticed that on some days it seemed to be a bit worse than others. "It must still bother 'im," she said to herself. But he never did comment on it.

The house was empty of little ones, they all being in school, and Missie was enjoying her teaching.

As soon as Clark was able he was at the logging again. The neighbor men, true to their word, had hauled out all the logs he had previously cut, but according to his calculations, he would still need another four wagon loads.

Marty watched him go with a feeling of anxiety and breathed a silent prayer of thanks when he returned safely at the end of the day.

Marty looked forward to spring. This was the summer of the promised new house. And having the building begun would take on special meaning, for once it was started, it would mark the end of Clark's daily trek to the woodlands.

It was an eventful summer. Marty watched as the new clapboard house took shape. It was even bigger than she had dreamed. There were a number of windows. A fieldstone fireplace graced not only the family living room and the parlor but the master bedroom as well.

Clark had obtained two men from town to assist with the building, so that even when he was busy in the fields, the work went on. Marty measured the windows and bought material for the curtains so that they would be ready to hang when the house was completed.

The house would not be ready by fall, but they planned to have their next Christmas in their new home. Nandry and Josh with little Tina, and a new family member by then, as well as Parson Joe and Clae would all be home to share the Christmas turkey with them. They could even stay the night if they wished, and body would not be tripping over body.

It was something grand to look forward to, and Marty spent many hours planning and dreaming.

# Chapter 44

## *Thet Willie*

Missie closed the exercise book she had been marking and heaved a contented sigh. It was hard to believe that she was already into her second year at the local school. She loved teaching. True, she had some rascals in her classroom, her own young brother Luke being one of them; but all in all she was glad that she had chosen to be a teacher.

She piled the books neatly together and got up to clean the chalkboard. Her back was to the door, so she didn't see the figure move stealthily in, and when a pair of hands circled 'round to cover her eyes, she screamed in alarm.

"Hey, hey, it's okay," a voice said, realizing that he had unintentionally scared her half out of her wits.

"I didn't mean to fright ya, only surprise ya like."

Missie looked into the face of Willie LaHaye. Through her mind flashed the dead mouse, the grasshopper, and the other pranks that Willie had played in the past. Her fright turned to anger and she swung around, stomping one small foot.

"Willie LaHaye!" she exploded, "when are you ever gonna grow up?"

She wanted to bite her tongue as soon as she had said it, for her eyes assured her that Willie LaHaye had indeed grown up—at least on the outside.

Broad shoulders rippled with muscles as he moved, bushy

sideburns showed what his beard would be were he not clean shaven, and Missie had to look up a good way in order to throw her fury into his face.

Willie only grinned, the same maddening, boyish grin.

Missie spun around on her heel.

"Well, now that you've had your fun, you can be leaving."

"But I came to see the new school marm," he said, not at all perturbed by her anger. "I think thet I could use a little help on my A B C's.

"A is for apple, B is for bait, C is for coyness—E is for Eve, and thet's about as far as I can git."

"You're not funny—besides you missed D."

"D," said Willie, "D—about the only thing thet I remember that started with D is—dear."

Missie was so angry that she considered throwing the chalk brush she discovered was still in her hand.

"Willie LaHaye!" she started.

"I know," said Willie, "I'm not funny. Actually I stopped by to give ya some good news."

"Like?" prompted Missie.

"Like—I'm leavin'."

"Yer what?"

"I'm leavin'. I'm goin' on further west." Willie was suddenly very serious.

"To where?"

"Not sure. Ya know when Pa settled here, he had been planning on goin' on further. Hadn't been fer Ma gettin' sick we would have gone on. Well, I always was a mite disappointed. I'd sorta like to see what's over the next hill. Pa's all settled in here now, and Nathan is married and settled in too, an' I suddenly got to thinkin' they don't need me around atall."

Missie had cooled down some and was willing to talk if Willie would be sensible.

"What does your pa think?"

"Haven't told 'im yet."

"When would you go?"

Willie shrugged. "Don' know—that depends on a few things."

"Like—?"

"Like Ma—she's still not well, ya know, an' other things. Thought maybe next summer—maybe."

"Not soon then?"

"Depends."

Missie turned back to her boards and finished erasing the day's lessons.

"How's the teachin' goin'?" Willie asked.

"Good," said Missie "—only I had to send Luke to a corner today."

"What'd he do?"

"He dipped Elizabeth Anne's ribbons in an inkwell."

"Spoil-sport."

Missie remembered her own ribbons being dipped in an inkwell.

"It's not smart," she said defiantly, "hair ribbons cost money."

"Reckon they do. I'd never thought about that."

"Well, I told Luke that he had to save his pennies to buy new ribbons for Elizabeth Anne."

"You're a smart teacher."

"Not smart—just—"

"Pretty?"

"Of course not. Look, if you're not going to talk sense, I refuse to talk to you."

Missie walked over to close the open window. It was stuck. It wasn't the first time that it had stuck.

"Here let me help."

Willie stood directly behind her and reached out for the offending window. Missie was imprisoned between his arms. Her face flushed. She dared not turn around or she would be face to face with him.

Willie didn't seem in any hurry to lower the window, though looking at the muscular arms, Missie knew that the problem wasn't inability.

"Can't you get it either?" she asked, her voice surprisingly controlled.

"It's stuck all right."

"Willie LaHaye!" she stormed swinging around suddenly; "you're a liar."

"Yeah," he said grinning as the window came effortlessly into place. And there was Missie standing within the circle of Willie's outstretched arms.

Before Willie could make a move, Missie ducked down and under, then stepped back a pace, her eyes flashing fire. Then she swung on her heel and grabbed her coat.

"Please see that the door is closed when you leave!" she hissed, and was gone.

# Chapter 45

## *Missie's Callers*

Missie had her first caller. Marty knew that it was bound to happen, and soon, but even so she was unprepared for it when it did.

Missie had been the youngest member of her small class at the normal school, and, though Missie never said so, a popular member as well. Occasionally Missie referred to this fellow student or that fellow student, but Marty had had no reason to feel that anyone was *special* for any reason. Then one day at her door appeared a tall, sandy-haired young man, very well groomed and properly mannered. An expensive-looking horse, appearing to have some racing blood, stood tethered to the hitchingrail.

"How do you do. My name is Grant Thomas. Would Miss Melissa Davis be in please?" His voice was most respectful.

Marty stammered. "Why—why, yes—she's in." She finally found her tongue and her manners. "Won't ya come in please?"

"Thank you. And are you Melissa's mother? She spoke of you often."

Marty was still flustered. "Thet's right—please step in. I'll call Missie—a—Melissa—right away."

Missie seemed pleased to see the young man. Marty watched carefully for signs of more than just pleasure.

Grant stayed to share supper with them and proved to be a quiet, yet intelligent, young man. Clark seemed to quite enjoy him, and Marty kept sending Clark silent warnings that he shouldn't encourage him too much.

He said that he planned to ride on into town before nightfall. Missie saddled Lady and rode part way with him. They visited and laughed as they rode, thoroughly enjoying one another, which made Marty feel funny little shivers of fear run through her. Missie was so young—only seventeen. "Please, please don't make me give her up yet."

When Missie returned she went to the pasture gate and turned Lady loose, brushing and fussing over her before she sent her on her way. When she stopped outside at the basin to wash her hands, she looked quite normal enough. She paused to admire Ellie's cushion top that the younger girl was making before coming into the kitchen. She came in humming to herself as she often did. Marty could hardly wait.

"This here Grant, don't recall ya sayin' much 'bout 'im."

"Not much to say. Let's see—"

Marty could already see Missie's trick coming—"throw Ma off with some facts, nonessential facts, but facts none the less." "He's three years older than me, an only child, his ma leads the Ladies' Aid and his pa's a doctor. His folks live in a big stone house on Maple Street, I believe, only about seven blocks from the normal school. They like to entertain, so they have Grant's friends—which includes almost everyone—over for tea, or tennis, or whatever. There."

Marty wasn't to be sidetracked so easily. "What I want to know is, are you one of Grant's friends?"

"Guess so."

"Special like?"

"Oh, Ma," Missie groaned, "how do you make a fella understand that you like him fine—but it ends there?"

"Did ya tell 'im?"

"I thought that I had before."

"An' this time?"

"I hope that he understands."

Missie moved on to her room and Marty kept her knitting

needles clicking. She must remember to speak to the boys and inform them that she wanted to hear no teasing about the young man who had called. She hoped that the fellow truly did understand. Poor Grant.

Marty was not to be at peace for long, for Lou Graham asked Clark for permission to call. Marty had no problem accepting Lou, but she still had trouble accepting the fact that Missie was growing up. Nandry and Clae had both been older than the norm when they received callers and married, and Marty had half hoped that Missie would follow their example. Perhaps Missie would have, but the young men seemed to have other ideas.

Lou sat in their parlor now. He and Missie were busy playing checkers. Marty noticed Missie deliberately lose. Missie was a good checker player and would never, without intention, be caught as she was. Lou's mind didn't seem to be too much on the game, however, so perhaps the young man had some excuse.

Clare, Arnie, and Luke found it difficult to understand why Lou did not choose to join them in pitching horseshoes as he always had in the past. The three boys were finally sent to bed still puzzling over the situation.

After checkers, Missie fixed cocoa and sliced some loaf cake. The adults were invited to join the young people at the kitchen table, and they found no difficulty in chatting with the young Lou.

Missie walked with Lou to the end of the housepath and waited as he untied his horse and left for home. They had grown up together and should have felt quite at ease in one another's company, but their new relationship had placed a bit of tension between them. Time would care for that.

"Will he be back?" Clark asked Missie when she returned to the kitchen.

"I expect so."

Marty felt that her voice lacked enthusiasm.

"Nice boy," she commented.

"Uh hum. All the Grahams are nice."

"Do ya remember when ya were gonna marry Tommie?"

Missie giggled. "Poor Tommie. He must have been embarrassed. I told just everybody that—but he never said a word about it."

"Well, thet's all long in the past," continued Marty. "Tom has his Fran now."

"And me?"

Marty looked up in surprise.

"That's what you're thinking, isn't it, Ma? What about me?"

"Okay," said Marty, "what about you?"

"I don't know," said Missie. "I think that I need lots of time to sort that out."

"Nobody's gonna rush ya." Clark expressed both his and Marty's feelings.

Lou continued calling. Missie was friendly and a good companion, but Marty noticed that she didn't show the bloom of a girl in love.

# Chapter 46

## *Disturbin' Thoughts*

Missie was about to leave the school building when the door opened and Willie came in.

"Should I have knocked?" he asked.

"Wouldn't have hurt."

"Sorry," said Willie. "Next time I'll knock."

Missie continued to button her coat.

"Come to think of it—guess there won't be a next tme."

Missie looked up then.

"I really came to sorta say good-bye."

"You're leaving?"

"Yeah."

"When?"

"Day after tomorra."

"You said that you weren't going until summer."

"I said thet it depended on some things, remember?"

"I—I—guess so. Is your mother better then?"

Willie shook his head. "Fraid not. I don't think thet Ma will ever be better." There was sadness in his voice.

"I'm sorry," Missie said softly; then, "How are you going?"

"I'm takin' the stage out to meet the railroad. Then I'll go by rail as far as I can. Iffen I want to go on, I'll buy me a horse or a team."

"What are you planning to do once you get there—pan for gold?"

Missie's sarcasm was not missed by Willie, but he chose to ignore it.

"Kinda have my heart set on some good cattle country. Like to git me a good spread and start a herd. I think I'd rather raise cattle than plant crops."

"Well, good luck." Missie was surprised that she really meant it, and how much she meant it.

"Thanks," said Willie. He paused a moment, then went on. "By the way, I have somethin' fer ya. Sort of an old debt like."

He put his hand in his pocket and came out with some red hair ribbons.

"Iffen I remember correctly they were a little redder than these, but these were the reddest red thet I could find."

"Oh, Willie," whispered Missie, suddenly wanting to cry. "It didn't matter. I—I don't even wear these kinds of ribbons anymore."

"Then save 'em fer yer little girl. Iffen she looks like her mama, she'll be drivin' little boys daffy, an' like as not she'll have lots of ribbons dipped in an inkwell."

He turned to go. "Bye, Missie," he whispered hoarsely. "The best of everythin' to ya."

"Bye, Willie—thank you—and God take care of you."

Missie wondered later if she had really heard the soft words, "I love ya," or had only imagined them.

Missie tossed and turned on her pillow that night. She couldn't understand her own crazy heart. One thing she knew. She'd have to face up to Lou—tell him honestly and finally that she wanted him as a friend but nothing more. But even with that settled, her troubled mind would not let her sleep. She reached beneath her pillow to again finger the red hair ribbons. That crazy Willie LaHaye! Why did he have to trouble her so, and why did the thought of his leaving in two days bring such sorrow to her heart? Was it possible that after all these years of fighting and storming against him, she had

somehow fallen in love? Absurd! But Missie couldn't convince
her aching heart.

She arose the next morning suffering from a loss of sleep
and hurried off to school, not in her usual good humor.

The news came with the Coffin children. Mrs. LaHaye had
died during the night. Somehow Missie made it through the
day. Her heart ached for Willie. He had dearly loved his
mother. What would he do now? Certainly he would not be
able to leave on the stagecoach on the morrow.

If only she had a chance to talk to him, to express her sorrow, and to take back some of the mean things that she had
said down through the years.

The day finally drew to a close. Missie announced that due
to the bereavement in the community, classes would be cancelled for the following day. She did not remain behind to
clean the chalkboards or tidy the small schoolroom but
slipped into her coat and hurried home.

That evening Lou came to call. It didn't seem quite right
to Missie that a young man should go courting on the eve of a
funeral, and her agitation made it easier for her to follow
through on her intention of putting a halt to the whole affair.

The next day a third mound was added to the cemetery by
the church. Missie stood with other mourners, the wind wrap-
ping her long coat tightly about her.

When the others went in to be warmed by hot coffee, Missie left the group and walked toward a grove of trees at the far
end of the yard.

She was standing there silently, leaning against a tree
trunk, when a hand was placed on her elbow. She did not even
jump. Perhaps she had been expecting him.

"Missie?"

She turned to him. "I'm sorry, Willie—truly sorry about
your ma." Tears overspilled and slid down her cheeks.

Willie lowered his head to hide his own tears, then brushed
them roughly away. "Thank ya," he said, "but I'm glad—sort
of glad—thet I was still here. It could have happened after I'd
gone, an' then—then I'd always been sorry."

"Are you still going?"

Willie looked surprised at her question.

"Well, you said it depended on your mother, and I didn't know how you meant—"

"I didn't say thet—entirely. I said it depended on other things, too."

"On what?" The question was asked before Missie could check herself.

For a moment there was silence; then Willie said with difficulty, "On you, Missie—on you an' Lou. Guess ya know how I've always felt 'bout ya. An' now thet you an' Lou are— well—friends, there's nothin' much fer me to hang 'round here fer."

"But Lou and I aren't—aren't—"

"He's been callin' regular-like."

"But thet's over. There was never much to it—only friendship, and last night I—I asked Lou not to call again."

"Really? Really, Missie?"

"Really."

Another silence. Willie swallowed hard. "Would there be a chance—any chance thet I could—thet I could call?"

"You crazy Willie LaHaye," said Missie, boldly reaching up and putting her arms around his neck. "Are you ever going to grow up?"

Willie looked deeply into her eyes to see if she was teasing him, and seeing there the love that he had hardly dared to hope for, he pulled her close in a tender embrace. Willie LaHaye grew up in a hurry.

# Chapter 47

## *Another Christmas*

True to Clark's promise, the new house was ready before Christmas and the moving in was completed, though the weather was quite cold. Willie LaHaye was a frequent guest at the Davises' home, and Marty and Clark both appreciated the young man. If they had to lose their Missie, they were glad that it would be to such a fine fellow.

But on Christmas Eve Willie unintentionally dropped a bombshell. It had been during a casual conversation with the men of the house. Josh had been telling of his plans to get a better grade animal for his pig lot, and Willie stated that that was the direction he wished to go—starting with a few really good cattle and gradually building his herd; but first he'd have to choose just the right land for the project. He hoped in the spring of the new year to leave on a scouting trip and take plenty of time in picking his land. After he had secured it, he would return for Missie.

Clark's eyes opened wide and Marty's head jerked up.

"Yer not plannin' on farmin' 'round here?" Clark asked.

"I'm not plannin' on farmin' at all," Willie answered. "Got me a real hankerin' to do some ranchin' instead."

"How far ya think ya have to go to find good ranch land at a price one could afford?"

"Few hundred miles, anyway."

Marty felt a sickness go all through her. Willie was heading farther west. Willie was also planning to marry her Missie. "Oh, dear God," she thought. "He's plannin' on takin' Missie away."

She slipped quietly out to the kitchen, hoping that no one had noticed her leave. She walked into the coolness of the pantry and leaned her head against a cupboard door.

"Oh, dear God," she prayed again, "Please help 'im git this silly notion out of his head. I wonder, does Missie even know 'bout it?"

It was Missie who followed her out and found her.

"Mama," she said, laying a hand on Marty's arm. "Mama, are you feeling all right?"

"I'm fine—fine," said Marty, straightening up.

"Is it—what Willie said?"

"Well, I will admit it was some kind a shock. I had no notion thet he had such plans."

"I should have told you sooner—"

"Then ya knew?"

"Of course. Willie talked about it even before—before we made any plans."

"I see."

"I should have told you," Missie said again. "I suppose Willie thought that I had."

"It's all right, Missie."

"It's—it's kind of hard for you, isn't it, Mama?"

"Yeah—yeah, I guess it is." Marty tried to keep her voice from trembling.

"I suppose," said Missie, "that you feel kinda like your own mama felt when you planned to leave with Clem."

"Now ya listen here," Marty wanted to say; "you're bein' unfair, throwin' thet up to me." Instead she said, "Yes, I guess it is."

For the first time in her life Marty thought that she could feel some of what her mother must have felt and why she had resorted to protests and pleadings. She had never been able to understand it before, but she could now.

"Yeah," she said slowly, "I guess that this is how she felt."

"But you loved Clem," prompted Missie, "and you knew that you had to go."

"Yes. I loved him."

Missie gave her a squeeze. "Oh, Mama, I love Willie so much. We've even prayed about this together. We can go on farther west. We can open up a new land together. We can build a school, a church, can make a community prosper and grow. Don't you see it, Mama?"

Marty held her little girl close. " 'Course I see it. 'Course. It's jest gonna take some gittin' used to thet's all. You go on back now. Me, I'm gonna catch me a little air."

Missie looked a little reluctant, but then turned back to the laughter coming from the family sitting room.

Marty wrapped a warm shawl closely about her shoulders and stepped out into the crisp night air.

The sky was clear and the cold emphasized the brightness of the stars above her. Marty turned her face heavenward.

"God," she said, "she's yer child. We have long since given her back to you. Ya know how I feel 'bout her leavin', but iffen it's in yer plan, help me, Father—help me to accept it an' to let her go. Lead her, God, an' take care of her—take care of my little girl."

## Chapter 48

# *Promises of Spring*

The Davises saw much of Willie LaHaye in the next few months. It seemed to Marty that he might just as well move in his bedroll. They liked Willie and approved of the relationship between him and Missie, but Marty knew that the time with Missie would be far too short; and with her away at the school all day, it was difficult to share her with Willie almost every evening.

Missie and Willie were full of plans and dreams. Willie spent his days talking to men who had been farther west, inquiring about good range land. He was advised by most to travel west to the mountains and then follow the range southward. The winter snows were not as deep there, concurred the men, and the range land was good. Willie was cautioned to make sure that he choose carefully with a year-round source of water supply in mind.

One evening Missie returned in from bidding Willie goodnight, and her *glow* was of a different sort than the usual. Her eyes sparked angrily and her cheeks were flushed in rage. She took a quick swipe at her cheek with the back of her hand in an effort to hide the tears that had been there.

Clark and Marty both looked up in surprise, but said nothing.

"Thet—thet—Willie LaHaye!" Missie fumed and headed upstairs to her bedroom.

They never did know what the quarrel had been about, but two evenings later it appeared to be well patched up, forgiven, and forgotten.

On the tenth of May, Willie left to seek his new land.

Missie had bidden him farewell in private. His excitement carried over, spilling itself upon her. She wanted to see him go to find their land to fulfill their dreams, but, oh, she would miss him, and there was always the slight chance that he wouldn't be coming back. He assured her that he would, but she had heard tales of other men who had gone, and because of sickness or accident never returned. She tried to shut out the black thoughts, but they refused to be banished.

Willie, too, had his doubts. The West was calling, but maybe he was doing this all wrong. Maybe he should marry first and they should go together; then there would be no need for separation. It might be harder for Missie—trailing around looking for a place that could be theirs. Land was not as easy to come by now as it had once been—at least not good land. It would mean living in a covered wagon for many months, perhaps. No, that was selfish. He'd go alone and then come back for Missie. Perhaps in the heat of the search, the months would pass quickly. He prayed that they would. In the back of his mind, begging to be brought forward and recognized, was the picture of Lou Graham. There were other neighborhood boys as well—and Missie was a very pretty girl. Could a lonely girl, left for months on her own, hold out against the attentions of would-be suitors? It made Willie feel a bit sick inside.

Missie, who walked beside him, her hand in his, pushed aside the thoughts of both of them when she spoke.

"It's gonna seem a long time, I'm afraid."

Willie stopped walking, turned her to him and looked deeply into the misty blue eyes.

"For me, too." He swallowed hard. "I hope an' pray thet they go quickly."

"Oh, Willie," cried Missie, "I'll pray for you every night— that—that God will keep you and—and speed your way."

"An' I fer you." Willie traced a finger along Missie's soft cheek. Missie buried her face against his chest and let the tears flow freely. He held her close, stroking her long brown hair, letting the curls slip through his fingers. A man wasn't supposed to cry. Well, maybe he wasn't yet a man, for he could no more stop the tears from coming than he could fly west.

It was time for Willie to go. He kissed her several times, whispered his promises to her again and again, then put her gently from him. He dared not look back as he hurried to his horse.

"He'll be back," Missie promised herself aloud. "He'll be back."

Willie's good-byes were not yet over. Zeke LaHaye accompanied his son into town and puttered around at last-minute fixings and unnecessary purchases. When the time finally came for the group to be off, Zeke stepped forward and gave his son a hearty handshake and some last-minute cautionary advice, as he knew the boy's mother would have done had she been there.

"Be careful now, son. Be courteous to those ya meet, but don't allow yerself to be stepped on. Take care of yerself an' yer equipment. It'll only be of use to you iffen ya look after it. Keep away from the seamy side of things—I not be needin' to spell thet out none. Take care, ya hear?"

Willie nodded, thanked his pa, and was about to turn to go when Zeke LaHaye suddenly cast aside all reserve and stepped forward to engulf his boy in a warm embrace. Willie returned the hug, acknowledging how good it felt to be locked in the arms of his father. The last thing that Willie remembered seeing as he turned to go was Zeke LaHaye, big and weathered, brushing a tear from his sun-tanned face.

# Chapter 49

## *Willie's Return*

The day of Willie's unexpected return nearly turned the house upside down. Marty was in the kitchen turning out a batch of bread when Luke skipped in.

Missie, who sat hemming a tablecloth, paid little attention to her young brother until he announced in a teasing singsongy voice, "Willie's comin'."

"Oh, Luke, stop it," said Marty. Missie was miserable enough without being taunted.

Luke became defiant. "He is *too* comin'—jest see fer yerself." And he pointed down the road.

Missie ran to the window. "He *is*, Ma!" she shouted, and left the house on the run.

"See there," said Luke and followed Missie out.

"Well, I be." Marty stood at the window and watched Willie's galloping horse slide to a stop and Willie leap to the ground, all in one motion.

"My word," said Marty her breath caught by Willie's recklessness. "The boy been all the way west and back and then risks his neck in my yard in a hurry to leave his horse."

As the young couple embraced, Marty turned back to her bread. In a way it was hard to believe that Willie had been gone almost a year. Marty had secretly looked forward to having the extra time with Missie all to themselves, but the look in Missie's eyes and the evidence of sleepless nights soon made Marty realize that she, too, would gladly welcome Willie's return. She still did harbor a small hope that Willie might have changed his mind in the meantime, or that the land he was looking for simply was not available.

There was a babble of excitement at the table that evening. Missie was full of questions; Willie was full of feasting his eyes on Missie. Clark and Marty hoped that some kind of information regarding Willie's trip would eventually be brought to the fore.

"Hear ya found yer land," from Clark.

"Sure did."

"What's it like?"

"Well, sir," Willie's eyes shone. "It's 'bout the nicest thing—land-wise," he quickly amended, "thet a man ever set eyes on."

"There's no tall timber in that area—only scrub brush in the draws. The hills are low and rolling with lots of grass. Toward one end is a valley—like a picture—with a perfect spot fer home-buildin'. It's sheltered an' green, with a spring-fed crik runnin' down below. Lotsa water on the place, too. Three springs thet I know of—maybe more thet I didn't spot out yet."

The shine in Willie's eyes was contagious.

"Almost makes me wish thet I wasn't old an' crippled, son," Clark quipped.

Marty reached out from where she stood behind his chair and touched his hair affectionately, assuring him that she considered him neither.

"Were ya able to make the deal?" Clark was a practical man. Searching out good land did not mean ownership.

"Thet's what took the time," said Willie. "Man, ya jest wouldn't believe the hassle—goin' here, goin' there, seein' this man, lookin' up thet 'un, sendin' fer government papers. I began to wonder iffen I'd ever git through it all."

He grinned. "Finally did though. The papers I hold declare it all to be mine. An' it's a lot closer ta here than I had expected it to be. Won't take too long at all to travel on out.

There's a couple of wagon trains thet travel through thet way every summer. Takin' supplies mostly to the towns down south, but they have no objection to travellers followin' along with 'im. Thet way ya git there safe an' sound with all yer supplies at hand."

So it would be by wagon that Missie travelled after all. Marty had secretly hoped that if she really had to go, there would be some other way. She crossed to the fire and began adding wood where none was needed. She checked herself. She'd be driving everyone from her kitchen with the heat.

No use trying to pretend anymore. Her little girl was leaving, going west, and in a very short time. She had not spoken out against it, but somehow she had pushed it aside, hoping that things would change—that the young couple would decide not to go. Now here was the excited young man, possessor of papers that declared him a landowner out west, and an equally excited Missie hanging on his every word as though she could hardly wait to get started. There was no stopping it now. Marty decided to slip quietly out for a little walk to the spring.

# Chapter 50

## *Ellen's Machine*

The wedding day drew nearer. The house was still caught in the activity of preparations. Careful consideration needed to be given to each item that Missie prepared for her new home, for it would need to stand the long trip by wagon to Willie's purchased land.

Marty had gone to her old trunk and produced a lace tablecloth that had been made by the hands of her own dear grandmother for her wedding gift. Most of the things that Marty had owned she had long ago put to use, but this was special. Also in the trunk was a spread that Marty's mother had made. This would be saved for Ellie.

Besides sewing the linens and the various other household needs, Missie was busy preparing her wardrobe. There was no way that Marty wanted her caught short no matter how long they should be on the trail. Her dresses had to be light for the hot summer ahead and yet serviceable for the time spent travelling in the wagon.

Missie sewed with enthusiasm. She enjoyed sewing and with a reason as exciting as she deemed hers to be, the job was a pleasure rather than a chore. Bright bonnets and colorful aprons took shape. Dresses were carefully sewn, then bundled and packed in stout wooden boxes that Clark had made. Marty kept thinking of things that Missie would need. Things that she herself had not had the foresight to pack when she came West. Pans, utensils, kettles, crockery, medical supplies, jars, containers for food—the list seemed endless and often left Missie laughing with an, "Oh, Ma."

Marty's troubled mind refused to find rest but continued to go over the same worn-out route again and again—no doctor, no preacher, no schools, maybe no near neighbors—which meant no Ma Graham. Oh, how she hated to see Missie go.

But Missie sang as she worked and packed and fairly danced through the house in her happiness.

At the sound of an approaching horse, Missie jumped up from the machine where she had been busy finishing a gingham dress.

"There's Willie. He promised me that he'd help me pick enough strawberries for supper. We won't be long, Ma."

Marty sighed and put aside her sewing to go make some shortcake to go with the berries.

The young people set off, arm in arm, for the far pasture, Missie's old red lunch pail swinging at Willie's side.

On the way to the kitchen Marty stopped and looked at Missie's sewing. She had become a good seamstress. Marty was proud of her.

She stood fingering the garment and then her hand lovingly travelled over the machine. All through the years since she had become Missie's mama, this machine had sewn the garments for each of her children. Clothing was mended, new towels hemmed, household items for three brides had been made here, young hands had learned the art of sewing. It was a good machine. It had never let her down. True, it didn't have the same shine that it had when it was first carried through her door, but it had borne the years well.

Marty was deep in thought, so she didn't hear Clark enter and was for a time unaware that he stood beside her.

Her tears fell unattended. She did not even seem to be aware that they were falling. He reached out and took her hand. She looked up at him then and shook herself free from her reverie. It was a moment before she felt controlled enough to speak.

"Clark, I been thinkin'. I'd like to give Ellen's machine to Missie. Ya be mindin'?"

It was silent for a time and then Clark answered. "It be yours to give. Iffen thet's what ya want, then it's fine with me."

"I'd like to—she'll be a needin' it in the years ahead. And Ellen *was* her mama."

"An' what will you do?"

"I can go back to hand sewin'. I was used to thet, but Missie—she has always used the machine. She'd be lost without it. 'Sides, I think thet it be fittin' like."

She brushed away the last trace of tears, ran her hand again over the smooth metal and polished wood of the beloved machine.

"Will ya be good enough, Clark, to make it a nice strong crate, an' then I'll wrap an old blanket around it so's it won't get scratched."

Clark nodded his head. "I'll git right to it tomorra."

"Thank ya," Marty said and went out to prepare the short-cake.

# Chapter 51

## *Thet Special Day*

Missie's wedding day dawned clear and bright. Marty had felt sure that it would. The day suited the girl—the happy, excited, pretty, young girl.

Marty paused a moment before leaving her bed to say a quick prayer. "Oh, God. Please, please take care of our little girl—an'—an' make today a day thet she can look back on with tears of joy."

There was so much to be done. Marty knew that she mustn't dawdle in sentimentalism. She dressed quickly and went to the kitchen. Clark was already up. A lively fire was burning in the old cookstove. When they had moved into the new house, Clark had declared that she could have a new cookstove—something more up-to-date—but Marty had refused.

"Why, I'd feel disloyal," she had explained, "castin' out a faithful ole friend like thet. We've boiled coffee together fer friends, baked bread together fer family, an'—an'—even cooked pancakes," she finished with a teasing smile.

So the old stove had moved with her. She checked the wood in it now and pushed the kettle forward.

Missie had decided to be married at home.

"I want to come down those stairs there on Pa's arm. Really, Ma, if you open up all of the rooms, it's most as big as the church anyway."

Clark and Marty had been happy to agree.

The morning hours flew by too rapidly. There were last-minute preparations of food for the afternoon meal. Fresh flowers needed to be brought in and arranged. Children needed to be checked on to see that they had done their assigned chores. Marty seemed to be on the run most of the day.

The wedding was set for three o'clock in the afternoon. It was after two before Marty was able to turn from the kitchen, do a last-minute check on her readiness, and hurry to her bedroom for a quick bath in the tub that Arnie had prepared for her. She slipped into her new dress. Her long hair tumbled about her shoulders and as she pinned it up, she noticed that her fingers trembled. After a last-minute check on her appearance, she went to Missie's room.

"Oh, Ma," Missie whispered. Marty thought that Missie had never looked prettier than at that moment. Standing there in her wedding gown, her cheeks flushed, her eyes moist with tenderness, she looked the picture of the glowing, happy bride. Marty's throat caught in a heavy lump.

"Yer beautiful, Missie," she whispered. "Jest beautiful." She pulled the girl close to her.

"Oh, Ma," sighed Missie. "Ma, I want to tell you something. I've never said it before, but I want to thank you—to thank you for coming into our lives, for making us so happy—me and Pa."

Marty held her breath. If she tried to speak she'd cry, she knew that, so she said nothing, only pulled her little girl closer and kissed the brown curly head.

Clark came in then and put his arms around both of them. His throat was tight as he spoke. "God bless," he said, "God bless ya both." He placed a kiss on the cheek of each of them and then he placed his hand gently on Missie, tried to clear the hoarseness from his throat and prayed in a low voice, "The Lord bless ya an' keep ya, The Lord make His face to shine upon ya, and be gracious unto ya; the Lord lift up His countenance upon ya and give ya peace—now an' always, Missie. Amen."

Missie blinked away happy tears and moved out into the hall to get last-minute instructions from Parson Joe.

Clark reached for Marty. At first he said nothing, only looked deeply into her eyes, willing her strength and peace for the hours ahead.

"It hurts a mite, doesn't it?" he whispered.

Marty nodded. "Isn't she beautiful—our Missie?"

Clark's eyes darkened. "Yeah, she's beautiful."

"Oh, Clark—I love her so."

"I know ya do." He pulled her close and his hand stroked her shoulder. "Thet's why yer lettin' her go."

Down below, the waiting neighbors were beginning a hymn. Marty knew that it was time for her to take her place. Soon Clark would be coming down the stairs with the radiant Missie on his arm.

She looked at Clark, silently accepting with appreciation the strength that he offered; then she slipped away.

She would not cry—not today—not on Missie's wedding day. There would be many days ahead for that. Today she would smile—would face her neighbors as the happy mother of the bride—would welcome, with love, another son.

She stopped at the top of the stairs, breathed a quick prayer, took a deep breath, and descended smiling.